JAYHAWKER

BY PATRICIA BEATTY

Be Ever Hopeful, Hannalee
Behave Yourself, Bethany Brant
Charley Skedaddle
The Coach That Never Came
Eben Tyne, Powdermonkey
(coauthored with Phillip Robbins)
Eight Mules from Monterey
Lupita Mañana
Sarah and Me and the Lady from the Sea
Turn Homeward, Hannalee
Who Comes with Cannons?

PATRICIA BEATTY

JAYHAWKER

11039

Morrow Junior Books
New York

Book design by Karen Palinko

Printed in the United States of America.

3 4 5 6 7 8 9 10

Library of Congress Cataloging-in-Publication Data
Beatty, Patricia, 1922–
Jayhawker / Patricia Beatty.
p.   cm.
Summary: In the early years of the Civil War, teenage Kansas farm
boy Lije Tulley becomes a Jayhawker, an abolitionist raider freeing
slaves from the neighboring state of Missouri, and then goes
undercover there as a spy.
ISBN 0-688-09850-9 (trade)
1. United States—History—Civil War, 1861–1865—Juvenile Fiction.
[1. United States—History—Civil War, 1861–1865—Fiction.
2. Slavery—Fiction.   3. Underground railroad—Fiction.   4. Spies—
Fiction.]   I. Title.
PZ7.B380544Jay   1992
[Fic]—dc20   91-17890 CIP AC

*For
my editor,
Andrea Curley*

Contents

Chapter One

THE BLESSING

*E*lijah Quentin Tulley, isn't it? I hear they call you
Lije."

The visitor's wild gray eyes bored deeply into twelve-
year-old Lije's, making him shudder with fear and excitement. The tall man's dark hair stood stiffly on end.
It looked to the still sleepy boy as if it had been smeared
with the ashes his mother used in her soap making.

The man went on in his booming voice as Lije's
parents stood mutely behind their son, while his
younger sisters, who had also been called down out of
the loft at midnight, cowered against the cabin wall.

1

"It would have been better for this boy if you had named him Joshua or David or Gideon—men who were fighters for the Lord. Soldiers are what we need today in Kansas Territory, soldiers for God."

Lije's father, a lanky, long-jawed, fair-haired man, said proudly, "Mr. Brown, that's exactly what we are, soldiers. That's what Lije'll be, too, once he gets his growth. He shows promise of being tall."

John Brown nodded. "It appears to me, Absalom, that he's coming up to that real fast. He's big already and going to be bigger. Tell me, Lije, are you planning on helping the cause of abolition here?" The man's deeply lined face darkened as he looked down at the boy. "Do you know what that sacred word means?"

Though frightened by the stark appearance of this awe-inspiring visitor, Lije got out, "Yes, sir. It means freeing slaves."

"That isn't all. It means that Kansas will come into the Union as a free state. It's the last days of this year of the Lord 1858. I say Kansas will enter this Union *free* by 1861—to balance out Missouri." Brown's fierce gaze held Lije's fast. "What's wrong over in Missouri, son?"

Lije knew the answer very well. "There are slave-owning men over there, Mr. Brown, sir. That's why us Tulleys come to Kansas Territory from Iowa—to live and farm here so Missourians can't bring slaves in and make this a slave state, too."

Brown nodded gravely. "And that's why Southerners flock into Missouri and come here to settle in Kansas Territory. They want to try by any foul means they can to plant the accursed wickedness of slavery on Kansas soil. But this must and shall remain free soil." The great abolitionist's deep voice rose to a bellow.

Lije stepped back, feeling the hair bristle at the nape of his neck. Brown was a roaring man.

"Don't you back off from me, boy. Your pa and your ma asked me to bestow my blessing on you and your sisters."

Pushed forward gently by his mother, Lije felt John Brown's big hand come to rest heavily on his dark red hair. The man cried out now, filling the cabin with his voice. "I dedicate this Kansas boy to be a true warrior like those in the Bible, a warrior of his people and a credit to his family forever."

Now he gave Lije a little shove and said, "It's growing late. We want our work over and done with by daylight, friend Absalom. Bring forth your daughters. I'll give them my blessings now."

Timidly, eight-year-old Clarissa and seven-year-old Emmajane Tulley crept forward to have their soft yellow heads covered by John Brown's two big hands as he muttered words over them. Then all at once the man whirled about and stomped out the cabin's only door.

Lije's father got his coat and hat from the nails beside

the door. As he put them on, he said, "Alice, see to it that the children go back up to bed. They'll take ill in just their nightshirts."

"Yes, Absalom." Mrs. Tulley's voice was soft. "I'll have coffee and hot corn bread for all of you when you get back. Good luck, my dearest."

Suddenly Alice Tulley came forward to embrace her husband. This was something Lije had seldom seen her do before. Her hands clutched at Absalom for a long moment, then swiftly let go. "Take care of yourself, Ab. Oh, God, you be careful! What you do is fearful work."

"The Lord's work," he corrected her. "It ain't as if I haven't done it before this night. You pray the way you generally do. If anybody comes asking for me, tell them I've gone to Lawrence overnight to buy a keg of nails."

Now Lije's father took down the shotgun from its rack, nodded to his silent, grave-faced family, went out, and shut the door.

Lije and his mother went to the window and watched as Absalom Tulley walked out into the blustery winter night to join Brown and his two sons, standing beside two wagons with harnessed horses. Quietly the men climbed up into the wagons, and a moment later they were gone.

After bolting the door, Mrs. Tulley ordered, "Go up to the loft, children. Say your prayers again and make sure you put Mr. Brown and his sons in them, along with your pa. Pray hard."

Halfway up the ladder behind his sisters, Lije asked, "They're going over into Missouri again, ain't they, Ma? Is there going to be a war over slavery pretty soon?"

The white-skinned, freckly woman who had given her son, Lije, her big bones and dark auburn hair, sighed. "We think there will be. Mr. Brown desires it. So do a lot of men. They ain't all abolitionists like him and your pa. Some are slave-owning men."

Lije asked, "Like the Missouri men, Ma?"

"Like all the states in the South. Get up to bed, Lije. Maybe when the men come back, you'll be called down again to help out."

Lije went up to his quilts, pulling them up to his chin to stop his shivering from cold and excitement. He lay on his back and stared at the darkness above him. He knew his mother would lower the flame on the kerosene lamp now and sit beside the stove all night long—longer if need be. Elijah Tulley sighed as the warmth of his quilts crept over him. To think he'd been introduced to John Brown, the famous abolitionist, and had been noticed by him, even called by name! He could still feel the weight of the great man's hand on his head. Maybe he always would. John Brown's blessing meant something wonderful. It was a summoning!

Clarissa's high little voice out of the darkness said, "Lije, that old man twisted my neck."

"Mine, too," whimpered Emmajane from their corner of the loft.

Lije grinned and said nary a word. What would they know, small as they were, about the remarkable thing that had just happened to them?

"Lije, Elijah, wake up!"

Because he'd slept fitfully from excitement, the boy came awake fast and sat up, pushing away his quilts. He could see his mother's face and head at the top of the ladder, illuminated by the light of the lamp she'd carried with her.

"Are they home yet, Ma?"

"No. Watchie's barking. It can't be them. Your pa would stop Watchie right off. I looked out. It's other men. No wagons—just horses."

Lije froze. That could mean only one of two things. Soldiers out hunting for John Brown, or men who'd ridden over from Missouri to look for him and maybe even burn the Tulleys out. "Bushwhackers" was what these Missourians were called in Kansas Territory.

"Who is it, Ma?"

"I don't know who they'd be. There's four of them. They just got down off their horses and are heading for the house. You stay up there and don't you say a word. Keep your sisters quiet, too."

"Ma, I want to come down."

"No. Leave them to me."

There was no polite rap on the door, but rather a battering sound that rang through the cabin like a falling tree branch in a storm. Lije scooted across the loft to his sisters' corner, put his hands over their mouths, and whispered into their ears, "You hush up, now. Ma says we got to."

Then he went over to another part of the loft and peered down through a crack in the boards. He watched his mother go with her lantern to the door, unbolt it, and lift the string latch.

Four booted, bearded men in heavy dark jackets filled the room at once. Two carried long pistols aimed at Alice Tulley. All four gazed around the cabin, taking in everything they could see in the dim light with their swift-flicking eyes.

The tallest of the men spoke sharp as a whip sounds. "I'd be Judah Hamilton. We're from Missouri. We come here looking for John Brown and his boys and for Absalom Tulley."

Another Missourian added, "We were told this be Tulley's land."

"It is." Alice Tulley's voice was steady, and she went on smoothly, making Lije marvel at her ability to lie. "My husband's gone to Lawrence on business. He's having a plow repaired there and he needs a keg of nails. He planned to stay overnight. You'll see if you

7

go to the barn that the team and wagon are gone. He took them with him."

"What about old Brown, ma'am?" The tallest spoke again.

The woman's voice stayed level and even, as if she were speaking to Lije about filling the woodbox. "John Brown ain't here. I didn't know he was even in the Territory. Put away your pistols. There's no one in the cabin but me and my son and the little girls up in the loft. Search here and in the loft and in our out-buildings. Search the well and springhouse, and the barn and woodshed, too. But if you go up to the loft, please don't frighten my children again. I'm sure you did when you beat on the door just now."

Another of the Missourians asked her, "Are you sure Brown wasn't here? Sometimes he goes by the name of Hawkins."

"No."

The leader took the lantern from Mrs. Tulley, climbed up the ladder to the loft, and shoved the light out at arm's length. Lije, now back in bed with his face hidden under the covers, saw only its glow, but he heard the man's voice saying, "There's some kids up here under some quilts, I'd say, and some cabbages and pumpkins, but that's all. There ain't no men hiding up here."

The tallest Missourian nodded. "We'll do what the lady says—have a look around. It'll go hard with you,

ma'am, if we find old Brown or his sons or any signs
of the mischief we figure he's up to. We know he's
back here in Kansas Territory again, and we got a rope
ready for his neck! Your man would do wise to keep
clear of Brown. We hear tell he took up with Brown
once before. You beware."

Lije, who'd come silently back to his crack, watched
his mother take the lantern and heard her say, "I'll tell
my husband. Good night to you."

The men slipped quietly outside to be greeted by a
barking Watchie. When they'd gone, his mother shut
the door behind them, then stood by the window,
keeping her eyes on them as they prowled about on
the Tulley property.

Lije moved to the opening to the loft and called
softly from above, "Ma, what if the bushwhackers run
into Pa and Mr. Brown and the others coming back
here?"

"Pray to God they don't come onto each other, Lije.
I'll set our lantern in the window that faces east. That
ain't where it belongs. Absalom told me to do that as
a sign to him if something goes wrong when he goes
away and comes home. It'll give him warning."

The boy saw his mother turn the flame up and
watched her set the lantern atop the cherrywood bu-
reau that had come by wagon from Iowa. It was her
finest possession, a wedding gift from her parents.

Now he watched her sit down at the table to wait

and listen for the welcome sounds which would announce that the Missourians had left. After what seemed like a very long time, he heard the jerking of bridles and the clomp of hooves and the renewed barking from their black-and-white dog. Lord be praised, they hadn't shot old Watchie.

His mother stood up and called to him, "Tell the girls to go back to sleep, Lije. Then you get dressed and come down. Give thanks they didn't burn us out or take whatever they wanted like they did in Lawrence years back when they raided the town."

As he pulled on his trousers, Lije growled to himself, "Curse all slave-owning Missourians."

He went over to his sisters, told them everything was all right again, and went down the ladder. The minute he was on the floor of the cabin, he asked, "Am I to keep you company, Ma? The gals are crying, they're so scared."

"They'll be all right. Yes, I'd like your company. I'll fix some hot milk for them and take it up. Lije, you children don't have to go to school in the morning. I'll write a note that you and the girls took sick in the night. It'll be a lie, and the Lord hates lies and liars, but it'll be in a good cause, and He'll forgive me for the sake of John Brown." As she poured milk from a pitcher into a pan to set on the stove, Alice Tulley asked, "Do you remember the first time you saw Mr. Brown, Lije?"

Remember? Lije lifted his dark brown eyes to his mother's. How could he forget even though he'd only been eight years old then? The Tulleys were hiding John Brown away in a brush shanty deep in the woods near the creek after he'd executed some Kansas men who had favored slavery and done harm to free-soil folks in Kansas. His pa had taken food and news to Brown, and Ma had done his washing, passing Brown's shirts off as her husband's laundry on the clotheslines. She'd felt honored to do that for Mr. Brown. Those days of hiding him had been frightening because of the lawmen and the men in army uniforms who were hunting for him and asking questions. They'd even stopped Lije as he walked to the one-room school a mile away and asked if he'd seen John Brown, showing sketches of him. Clarissa and Emmajane had never known he was there near the creek, but Lije knew who the man calling himself Mr. Hawkins really was. He'd been awake that night and looked through the crack in the loft when the fiery abolitionist had come at midnight, asking the Tulleys for shelter. He'd heard his pa promise it to him, sounding proud. And the next morning he'd worked with Pa, cutting brush to make the shelter.

Brown had come to them then wounded, with grape-shot in his back. Ab Tulley had cut the pellets out and bandaged the wounds, while he, Lije, had stood along-side them, marveling that Brown had not once cried out. How brave he'd been and how just he was to avenge what rampaging Missourians had done to the town of Lawrence.

Lije asked, "Ma, how come you waited till he came here again to ask Mr. Brown to bless us kids?"

Alice Tulley managed a smile. "Because you and the girls weren't old enough then to know what being blessed by John Brown means. You do now."

"I sure do, but the girls don't."

"You can tell them the rest of their lives, Lije. Mr. Brown wants you to be a soldier of the Lord like your pa, and to stamp out slavery."

Lije asked, "Are Mr. Brown and his sons going to hide out here when they return?"

"Not if they come back safe tonight with what they set out after. Mr. Brown won't want to stay here. He'll go on. He has plans, great ones, that will take him to the East Coast. He came to Kansas again to do the Lord's work at the call of his sons. He's still wanted by the law. He told your pa that when he leaves Kansas, we won't ever see him again, but he promises we'll be hearing about him and his deeds. And we will, too. He keeps his word. He says he'll start a war, a holy one." Mrs. Tulley sighed. "Wars take lives, even holy ones. I think the milk's warm now, and I'll take it up to your sisters. Put your head down on the table, son. Fold your arms and try to get some sleep. You can barely keep your eyes open. I plan to sit here and pray. If I could have the lamp nearby, I'd read the Bible, but the lantern's where it's most needed tonight."

His mother's hand tugging at his arm awakened Lije for the third time that night. She whispered, "They're back. Praise be to the Lord they came back. I heard your pa's special whistle to Watchie not to do any barking."

Lije went at once to the window that faced the east. Yes, in the dawn's dark gray December mist he saw the outlines of two wagons. His heart leaped with gladness. It was Pa, along with John Brown and his sons, but no others! Flinging on an old buckskin jacket of his pa's, Lije ran outside while his mother stirred up the cookstove fire. Soon there'd be water boiling for coffee and corn bread baking in the oven.

"Pa, Pa, the Missouri men came here," cried Lije as he caught at the harness of the wagon horse closest to him. "Did you see them anywhere?"

"No, son, thank the Lord. Did the bushwhackers hurt you or your mama or the girls?" came Absalom Tulley's voice, husky with anger.

"No. Ma told them you went to Lawrence. They searched around here, and then they left. Did you fetch what you went after?"

"We sure did, son. There's six in this wagon under

the blankets and five more in Brown's. There wasn't
any killing done to get them, either. Take a look."

Lije quickly climbed up over the wagon wheel onto
the seat and then down into the bed. He drew back
the blankets. What he found surprised him, but then
he understood. Six faces, frightened-looking black
ones, stared back up at him. There were two men, two
women, and two small girls.

"Don't you be scared," Lije told them fiercely.
"You're in Kansas Territory now. You're free! My pa
will hide you in the woods, and Mr. Brown'll take you
north when he goes. Come out and my ma will feed
you something hot."

As fast as he'd climbed onto the wagon, Lije scram-
bled down to the ground. He was about to run and
get his mother when he saw something that stopped
him in his tracks and held his gaze.

The ex-slaves in John Brown's wagon had gotten
down by now and surrounded the man. The two
women, one old, one young, were weeping on one
another's shoulders. Suddenly, one of the men, the
older one of the two, sank to his knees. He caught
hold of John Brown's hand, kissed it, and then cried
aloud, "Moses!"

Moses? Lije's thoughts went to the Bible. Moses had
led his people out of Egypt, where they'd been slaves,
and to the promised land as a free people. Yes, John

14

Brown did look like Moses or some other hero from the Bible, standing gaunt and tall in his long, gray duster coat with his hand on the slave's head.

Long as he lived, Elijah Tulley would never forget this sight. He'd treasure it forever in his memory as he would John Brown's blessing.

Chapter Two

NEWS FROM
VIRGINIA

O nce he'd heard that the Missouri men had come
seeking him, John Brown didn't stay long. He
waited till the black people had had coffee and hot
buttered corn bread. Then he ordered them all into his
wagon and got up onto the seat beside one of his sons.

He addressed the Tulleys standing below. "The Lord
thanks you, and I thank you for what you did for me
and for these black people. They'll be going north to
safety from slave hunters on the Underground Railroad
once I cross over with them into Nebraska. You did
right, Absalom Tulley, in helping me. It will be a star

in your heavenly crown. Come forward and shake my hand. I won't be seeing you again."

Now he reached down from the wagon seat and shook first Lije's pa's hand, then Alice Tulley's, and finally Lije's.

Afire with admiration, Lije found the courage to say, "I wish I had been named a Bible warrior's name, like you said."

Brown nodded, but did not smile. "When you are called upon to do the Lord's work like your pa here, take the name of Joshua. We don't use our own names in our holy work, you know."

Although Lije didn't know what the man meant, he replied, "I will, sir. I'll be Joshua. I'll remember."

"You do that, boy," said Brown, and with his son's crack of the whip over the team, the great evangelist left Kansas Territory.

The Tulleys stood for a long time watching him move off in the dawn's light. Finally he disappeared into the mists that arose from the creeks all around.

Ab Tulley sighed. "We won't see him again, but the whole country's going to hear from him mighty soon. It may take him some time to do the job. I'd like to tell you what he plans to do, but it's best you don't know."

After John Brown had gone, Lije unharnessed the team, weary after their cold December night's work in Missouri, rubbed them down in the barn, and led them to their mangers for their well-earned hay. Then he hastened to the cabin, where his father was lying, fully dressed, on the bed in one corner.

He found Absalom Tulley wide-awake, talking to his wife. His father talked and talked of John Brown as if the man was a fever on him. Sitting at the table, surprised at what he was hearing, Lije drank in whatever he could hear of the great man. He learned that his pa and Brown had picked up the slaves at a farm outbuilding where they'd gathered, waiting. Word had somehow been sent to them to go there and expect somebody from Kansas to come for them. Somebody had—the greatest abolitionist of them all!

On and on Absalom talked until Alice Tulley pulled a quilt up to his chin and said, "Hush, Ab. It's over now. You get some rest. We'll have a good Christmas now."

And then his father fell asleep at once.

Mrs. Tulley said, "He's worn down, Lije, tuckered all to nothing. He'll sleep a long time now."

"What if the men from Missouri come back?"

"We'll tell them he took a fever in Lawrence and came home sick. There's nothing to show there've been two wagons here. The ground won't show two sets of tracks because it's raining hard now. That'll make it all mud between here and the barn."

Lije burst out, "Ma, when Pa goes out next time, I

want to go with him. I ought to go. John Brown said I was to go."

"You ain't big enough and old enough yet." Alice Tulley touched his arm and shook her head. "Besides, John Brown gave your pa a name to remember before he left, one he can use."

"A Bible one, like Joshua or Gideon?" asked the boy.

"No, the name of a man from these parts who'll go over to Missouri with him."

"Who'd he be?"

"It's wisest you don't know. That's safest."

"Did Pa tell you his name?"

"No, and I won't ask him. Don't you neither. Now go rest. I won't be waking you for school tomorrow."

It was still raining when Lije shepherded his sisters to the one-room school two days later. Halfway there he was joined by one of his schoolmates, Ira Cousins, who lived on a farm nearby. While Lije would someday be a big man, Ira was undersized and always would be.

Ira was dressed like Lije, in a heavy woolen jacket with a scarf over his peaked hat, and wore mittens. He skidded along in the wet, slick grass beside Lije rather than tramp in the mud the way the other boy did.

"Hey, Lijah," came his hoarse whisper as he trailed the bigger boy. "I hear tell you had company night afore last at your place. I heard a Mr. Judah Hamilton came calling on you."

Although Lije had not expected this, he thought fast and after only a moment said with a laugh, "If we did, I slept right through it. When I'm sleeping, I wouldn't hear the old angel Gabriel with his trumpet." Then he asked, "Who's supposed to have come calling on us?"

"Some Missouri bushwhackers. One of them was named Hamilton."

Lije shrugged. "Maybe so. Maybe they just lost their way and came to Pa for directions. Maybe they wanted to know where the water was lowest in the crick that runs past our place so they could go home without getting too wet."

Ira stepped down into the mud to walk beside Lije. "Oh, they came, but it wasn't to ask directions. They was out hunting for old John Brown. They told my ma and pa who they was and that Brown was here and up to devilment again. Folks say John Brown never has to sleep at all and is up and busy all night long. Did you see him, Lijah?"

Lije scoffed. "Me, see John Brown? John Brown don't mess with kids like you and me. John Brown's a great man. He'd look right through the pair of us, like we wasn't there at all. He's got important work to do. Land's sake, Ira, all I do when I don't go to school is milk the cows two times a day, help Pa plow, plant corn in the spring, weed it, cut it, shuck it for fodder, and husk it for meal. That's all you do, too. What would John Brown see in you and me?"

"I know all that, Lije. My pa and ma are for abolition, too, like Mr. Brown. I jest thought maybe you got a gander at him. There's talk around here that he went to Missouri night afore last and fetched back black people and killed one slave owner in Missouri. Would your pa know about them things? He's known as a man powerful for abolition."

A Missourian had got killed on Brown's raid? Lije's face darkened. He hadn't been told that. Silent for a moment, he then told Ira, "Pa hates the slave hounds over there. It ain't no secret. Some folks around these parts say they're against slavery when they truly ain't. That ain't the Tulley way, and you know it. Come on. We'll be late for school, and you know our teacher keeps an ax on her desk."

Lije's longer stride took him ahead of Ira as he hurried to catch up with his sisters, so he scarcely heard Ira's next words. "I sure wish I could set eyes on John Brown. It'd be something to remember."

"It surely was," Lije said to himself, shivering. Why hadn't Pa told him about the dead Missourian?

Coming alongside the girls, who were talking about catching prairie dog pups for pets, Lije warned, "Don't you let out one peep about who came to see us night afore last."

"Oh, we sure won't," promised Emmajane, twisting

her sodden shawl to one side and letting the rain beat on her upturned face. "Me and Clarissa know that if we do, he'll come back to do something fearful to us. He scared us plenty, even more than Pa or the teacher does."

Lije agreed. "He'll scare plenty a folks in this country before he's done. He's a great man."

Except for hearing that there was a two-hundred-dollar reward to the person who captured him, there was no news of John Brown the rest of that winter. It was obvious to the Tulleys that his slave-filled wagon had made it safely to the North or they would have heard of his capture. As Absalom Tulley told Lije shortly after Christmas, "The Missourians would come over here to crow about it if Brown hadn't got clean away. They'd hang or shoot him on sight, then take them slaves back into servitude. They'd be sure to let those of us in Kansas who hold with abolition know what they did. It'd please them plenty."

Lije had wanted to ask his pa who had killed the Missourian on the raid, then decided not to. What good would knowing that do? He hoped, though, that it had been John Brown or one of his sons, not his own pa.

Spring passed with the Tulleys clearing and planting another acre of corn under cloudy white skies. The sow gave them nine little pigs and the cow a heifer calf.

Thickets by their creek grew green tipped while the hickories and walnuts and oaks put on their leaves.

Later in the season, Lije hoed corn, casting aside rapidly growing weeds with the heavy hoe that gave him muscles.

The early summer went by in long, hot days of going out with empty lard pails for berries and green plums with his excited sisters, who ahead of time had thoughts of the deep-dish lard crust pies their ma would make from them. They never drank the wine she made from the wild grapes, and neither did Lije, of course, but he was proud that he and the girls had picked them when his pa and callers to the house praised the wine as "Just dandy, Mrs. Tulley."

One sweltering July night during the dark of the moon, Lije awakened to the sound of wagon wheels. He sat bolt upright. Was his pa going over into Missouri? Was it somebody coming too late to visit? He peered through the crack and spied his mother setting the lamp in the window. Pa was leaving. Was he going alone? No, there came a man's voice calling softly to him, "All right. I'm ready, Ab. Let's go."

Lije caught his breath. He knew the deep, grating voice. It was Jacob Cousins', Ira's pa. Lije had only met him a couple of times, but his voice was unusual. He was Pa's partner, the man John Brown had told him about. No wonder Ira knew so much.

Now Lije heard his mother at the bottom of the

ladder. She must have heard him shifting around as he woke up. "Don't come down, any of you. Go back to sleep."

Lije didn't go back to sleep. He heard his pa and Mr. Cousins return near dawn. Not one word was said of the errand at breakfast, and Lije guessed it had been successful only from his pa's smile. They'd brought slaves over, and probably Jacob Cousins was hiding them or had taken them to free soil already. Nebraska wasn't far away.

Just before the corn was harvested in early September, the Tulleys received the first news of Brown. A stranger came riding to their cabin. He was elderly, tall, and thin. His coat, trousers, and boots were brown with dust. From the door Lije heard his sharp, hard, twanging voice speaking to his pa as he reined in his horse. Lije had never heard such an accent before. It wasn't soft and flat like his own.

"Would you be named Absalom Tulley?" the stranger asked.

"I would, and who would you be?"

"Nobody whose name you need to know, save that I am from Massachusetts. A friend told me that you, he, and I see eye-to-eye on certain matters. He asks that from now on, whenever you go to Lawrence, you buy newspapers that contain news from the East, especially from Virginia."

24

Lije saw the interest leap into his father's eyes. Then he shook hands with the man and said, "Won't you light for a spell and take supper with us?"

"I thank you, but I have other places to visit."

"Not over in Missouri?" asked Tulley with a laugh.

"Not in Missouri. I am not welcome there. Farewell to you." With that, the man spurred his horse and left.

Lije ran to his father. "I heard, Pa. Was that about John Brown? Was that man an abolitionist, too?"

"I'm sure it was. Our visitor had the proper handshake. Old Brown's up to something back East. Each time we go to Lawrence now we'll be getting a paper. Brown's busy—busy like he said he'd be. He ain't one to rest." Ab Tulley eyed his son up and down, grinned, and told him, "You're shooting up fast, getting most of your growth now while most boys your age are still sprouts. I doubt if John Brown would know you now, you've shot up so." He tousled Lije's hair. "But he might recall your hair. Not many folks got that color of red. Go see your ma and ask if she wants the woodbox filled."

Lije sighed. Chopping wood and hoeing corn were not his favorite chores. Working with the horses was. Nothing gave him the joy that riding did. Astride a horse, a man was something special!

On a trip to Lawrence for horse liniment, flour, and calico, late in October, the Tulleys got the news for which they had been waiting. They rode in just before noon to find Lawrence in excitement. Men and women were walking up and down its chief street, talking, nodding at one another, and going on to a different group to talk. A man came up to Ab as they entered the town off the ferry over the Kansas River. He asked, "Have you got the big news from the East yet? We had a rider come from St. Louis with it yesterday."

Before Absalom could ask about it, the man said, "John Brown led raiders to Harpers Ferry in Virginia on the sixteenth of this month. He got hold of the federal rifle works, and the army arsenal where they keep the guns. He plans to arm slaves all over the South so they'll rise up and set up a government of freedmen. Ain't that remarkable? There's another rider just rode in from St. Louis. He's over at the newspaper office right now. He'll have news, too. That's where I'm bound."

"Oh, my God, Brown's done it, thank God!" exclaimed Ab Tulley. He turned to Lije. "Let's get to the newspaper office and see what the latest news is. The news we just got was nine days old. It's already the twenty-fifth."

The little office was surrounded by a crowd of people streaming in, more and more by the moment, wild to hear more of Brown. He was a man many of them admired, for Lawrence was an abolitionist town. It had been founded by them. It was attacked and plundered and set fire to by angry, slave-holding Missourians just three years back, but it had been rebuilt speedily. The crowd did not make way for the Tulleys after they dismounted and tethered their horses. They had to push through the throng.

"How's it going, Jonas? What's going on at Harpers Ferry now?" Absalom Tulley asked a Lawrence merchant that he knew by sight.

Jonas shook his head. "Dunno yet, Ab. There's just been another rider come. The editor of the paper come out for a minute to tell us the Virginia militia have surrounded Brown. Sure wish we had the telegraph. Two of Brown's sons got killed. Right now the U.S. Marines from Washington, D.C., are storming the fire engine house where Brown's holed up. There's a colonel named Robert E. Lee leading them. We figure there's a third rider coming soon, so we plan to hang around. Everything we hear is days old, of course."

"Marines after Brown?" Ab Tulley breathed. He shook his head sadly and looked down at his worn boots.

Lije waited beside his father for the next rider, wondering how long that would be. He cracked his knuckles, remembering Brown and his blessing, and listened to men around him speak of Brown's great plans and the terrible trouble he was now in. Brown had aimed too high, they said. He'd been a fool to attack Harpers Ferry. Had he figured he could hold it against the militia and the Marines?

Finally Lije went across the street, and later his pa joined him. They sat silently for hours watching the newspaper office. They figured riders would keep coming one after another with important news like this.

They waited and waited till near sundown, when a dust-covered horseman came galloping from the south. He flung his lathered horse's reins to a man standing on the porch of the newspaper office and staggered inside the door. A few moments later, a big man, the newspaper editor, came out onto the porch, held up his hands, and called for quiet. Lije and Ab Tulley hurried over at once. The crowd hushed and let the editor speak in a high, excited voice. "It's real bad news from Virginia, my fellow citizens. It happened on the eighteenth. The Federals busted into the firehouse, killed two of Brown's raiders, and wounded Brown! They got him. That's the latest word. I'll write it all up for tomorrow's paper."

"Got him?" Lije softly asked his pa. "What'll they do to him?"

"Try him in a court and hang him. That's what they've wanted to do all along." Ab Tulley shoved his way back through the crowd, past weeping women with their aprons to their faces, spat in the dirt, and walked off, his head hanging down.

Lije copied his pa's every action. Together they walked to the store, leading their horses, his own red bay, Banner, which he'd raised from a colt, and his pa's chestnut, Flitch. The Tulleys tethered the animals, went inside, and stood at the counter.

The clerk, who'd just come in from the newspaper office, too, went behind the counter, slammed it down, and said with sour deliberation, "The Federals got old John Brown. They'll hang him for sure."

"I reckon so," agreed Ab Tulley.

"Well, Brown did take the law into his own hands, and no man can do that and get away with it."

"I reckon so. Lije, we'll take the news home to your ma now. There ain't no cause to wait for any more riders." Lije caught the grave look his pa gave him. He'd talk more openly on the way home.

Riding out of Lawrence at a jog trot, Ab Tulley rode his chestnut close to Banner. A flour sack and half a bolt of yellow calico were tied behind his saddle. Liniment hung from a cloth bag at Lije's pommel.

Once they had passed the last straggling wooden house before the ferry, Ab Tulley reined in and opened up. "Elijah, don't you grieve for Mr. Brown. When we were together, he told me what he had in mind to do. He wanted to do something the whole country would hear about, and he did it. He pretty much expected to be caught and knew he'd be found guilty and would get hanged."

"Pa, he wants to die!"

"He does. He wants to be a martyr, a sacrifice, and a famous one. He wants folks who hate slavery to remember his name and keep on with his work."

"Are we Tulleys going to?"

"You bet, but that ain't all Brown wanted. He wants a war over slavery."

"Is he going to get it?"

"Most likely he will. Southerners consider black men and women property, like horses and mules that can be bought and sold. Would you fight if somebody told you you had to turn Banner here loose so he could go wherever he wanted to?"

"I sure would."

"Well, so will the South, 'cause the North doesn't want it to have slavery. John Brown's name is going to be a battle cry for the North. You wait and see."

"He blessed me." A thrill of excitement ran through Lije from his boot heels to the top of his head.

"You bet he did, Elijah."

"And he said I ought to be called Joshua."

"So he did."

"Can I be a conductor on the Underground Railroad, like you are, Pa? Somebody who helps slaves escape to the North?"

"You could be, sooner than you think. Lots of Kansas folks ain't going to like hearing what'll happen to John Brown and hearing the Missourians crowing.

They'll want to hit back, and slave raiding's going to be a good way to do it."

Lije said, "I can ride real good, and Banner's a good horse."

Tulley warned, "You got to be able to defend yourself. You got to shoot straighter than you do before we ever take you over to Missouri."

"Who's we?" asked Lije, riding closer, expecting to hear Jacob Cousins' name.

"You'll find out when the time comes."

Greatly daring, Lije told his father, "I know Jake Cousins went out with you last summer. I heard him call to you and recognized his voice. I never told his son or even Ma that I know who your partner is. Clarissa and Emmajane slept through your going and coming back that night."

Ab Tulley nodded. "It's good that they did. I'm glad you know it—saves me telling you, don't it? And you did right to keep that to yourself. Jake's the one I go with. John Brown gave me his name."

Lije asked, "Pa, when'll they kill Mr. Brown?"

"He won't live to see Christmas of this year, son, mebbe not even December. They'll hang the brave men who went with him to Harpers Ferry, too, but there's others to carry on for them. This land'll be putting an end to slavery one way or another. You'd best start right now improving your marksmanship with my rifle and pistol."

31

Lije voiced, "I'll go practice down at the creek soon as we get home. I'll get good at it fast. I promise you, Pa."

Jake Cousins, a small man with a scanty dark beard, brought the Tulleys the next news about John Brown. He came riding through a light snowfall at sunset on December 3, dismounted, and came in to warm himself and drink some just-parched coffee. Being polite, he refused sugar, knowing how very much it cost. He'd never come calling before, so Lije figured he had something to say, though he didn't take off his coat.

Cousins took his time saying it. He held his steaming cup for a time to warm his hands, blowing on the scalding liquid.

Then he opened up, speaking deeply, harshly. "I just come from seeing the doc in Lawrence about a tooth that troubles me. I figured I'd better get it pulled out before we get snowed in. While I was there, the news came in about John Brown. They hanged him after a real short trial in Charles Town, Virginia." He sighed. "The others with him will hang before the month's over."

Alice Tulley bowed her head. "God have mercy on their souls."

Ab Tulley asked, "Whose souls? Brown and his sons

or the other ones? Him and his sons don't need it."

She shook her head. "I mean the souls of the men who killed Mr. Brown and the men who will rejoice in his being dead."

"Amen to that," rasped Cousins, sipping the coffee and making a face against its hotness.

Chapter Three

THE SKIES DARKEN

*A*ll of eastern Kansas prayed that the remainder of the 1860 winter wouldn't be like the blizzard year of 1856, when the Territory's cattle froze to death by the hundreds. The Lord was merciful and heard their prayers this year. Though the weather was bitter enough with ice and snow, winter passed without quail freezing in the hedges or frozen ears and tails dropping from the dogs, cats, and cows. That winter had been a dreadful time when starving wolves fought with the dogs at the cabin doors.

Ab Tulley and Jake Cousins did not go to Missouri

that winter nor in the early spring. Lije knew the reason. His ma was going to have a baby, and Pa didn't want to leave her and have her worry just now.

The baby started coming one morning when the ironwood tree had just bloomed with its bright pink blossoms. Peppery little Mrs. Cousins had promised to help when it was time for somebody to ride over and tell her.

That morning, while it was still dark, Alice Tulley told them all from the bed, "Birthing is a woman's job. There's nothing for the four of you to do here after Mrs. Cousins comes. So go on, all of you. You three get on to school. And you, Pa, keep chopping logs for the new cabin part. That'll keep you out of the way. Stay in earshot, though. If I want you, you'll get called. When the baby's come, we'll hang an apron on the clothesline so you'll all know. If you don't see the apron, you young 'uns stay in the barn when you come home from school."

As Lije saddled Banner to leave for Mrs. Cousins', his pa shooed the girls off to school, after braiding their hair with big, clumsy hands.

Lije asked his father, "Will Ma be all right?" He paused in his tightening of Banner's cinch strap.

"Well, why shouldn't she be? She birthed the three of you just fine, so she knows what it's all about by now. Get on with you, Lijah." Tulley nodded as he walked away with his ax over his shoulder, then turned back to say, "I want a real nice place for my family. Someday I plan to make a fine place with a veranda and five rooms, a stable and storage barn, an orchard out back, and an osage orange hedge that'll keep the pigs from rooting close to the house. Your ma hates them doing that."

Hearing this made Lije grin. She surely did. She didn't mind the chickens scratching about, but the hogs, no sirree!

Sarah Mae Cousins came riding behind Lije on Banner and, after a wave to Ab a distance away, went directly into the cabin. Lije continued on, riding Banner to the one-room schoolhouse presided over by a tall, gaunt, hard-voiced woman. She was a no-nonsense schoolmarm whom Lije and the other big boys respected. They never argued with her or sassed her back. She whipped with a switch only on Fridays. That was the day to be really wary.

Ira whispered once from his seat, "Lije, does your ma want a boy or a girl? Ma said the baby was due any minute."

"It is," Lije whispered back. "I fetched your ma a little while ago. We don't care what it will be. A baby'll do us fine." Then, aware of the teacher's hard, dark eyes on him, Lije lapsed into safe silence.

The boys could talk together more at recess, and they did. Ira met Lije under a hickory tree and asked,

"When do you think your pa and mine'll go out together again?" By now the boys trusted each other and
spoke often, but secretly, of their fathers' raids.

"When the creeks go down, I reckon. A horse can
swim across when they're up, but Pa says a wagon's
trickier to get over, and a loaded one trickier yet.
Mebbe in a month or so."

Ira nodded. "Pa says you might get to go next time,
too. I overheard him tell Ma. Your pa's been bragging
about your shooting good now and being so big for
your age."

A pleasant heat rose in Lije's cheeks. Pa bragging on
him? That was something new. Well, he had practiced
his marksmanship two hours a day all winter long. He
was hitting the tree stumps that he aimed at more and
more often. The old water elm and white oak were
both pitted with rifle and pistol bullet marks.

That day the teacher talked about the government
of the United States. There was going to be an election
come the fall, one of the most important ones the
country had ever had. She talked about the candidates
for President, Stephen Douglas and Abraham Lincoln.
The first man stood for keeping black slaves as property, and the second one was against slavery.

"Lincoln, Abraham Lincoln," Lije said over and over
to fix the name in his mind. He'd ask Pa about Lincoln
once he got home and found out about the baby. He'd
sure have his eyes peeled for that apron.

Eager as he was, Lije walked Banner beside his sisters so they would all get home together. When they came in sight of the cabin, Banner trotted and the girls ran. Then everyone stopped. There was no apron on the line!

Mrs. Cousins didn't come out of the front door at Lije's call. His pa did. Ab Tulley's face was long and set in harsh lines. He walked to his children and told them in a cracked voice, "Your ma is all right, but the baby didn't live longer'n two dozen breaths. He came into the world too puny. Go see your ma, but don't pester her. She's wrung out. Miz Cousins got our supper for us before she walked home. Don't talk to your ma about the baby. Miz Cousins baptized him John Brown Tulley. That's how I buried him in the woods. A preacher'll come out later on from Lawrence to say words over him."

Tears stung Lije's eyes as he went inside to see his mother, who lay abed. The white of the pillow wasn't much whiter than her face. She touched the girls' hands, then Lije's, and said weakly, "I told Ab I want to go to church in Lawrence some Sundays now. It's only ten miles from here. He promised me we'd go."

"Sure, Ma, we will," promised Lije, who choked, spun around, and went outside to his waiting father. He said, "We won't go to Missouri till she's better, will we?"

"No, we'll get the summer and harvest over first. Other men are going over."

Lije caught the fact that his pa had not corrected him when he'd said "we." Absalom Tulley went on, "No, we'll stay here for a spell."

"Pa, have you ever heard of a man called Abraham Lincoln?"

Tulley shook his head. "No."

"He wants to be President. He's against slavery."

"Then we'll pray he gets to be, Lije." Tulley nodded, looking into the fading sun. "If Lincoln gets elected, we can expect war. That could stop the raiding, but mebbe not. We'll have to wait and see, won't we?"

Alice Tulley regained her strength slowly that spring. By early summer she was going to church every other Sunday with either Ab or Lije driving the team. Clarissa and Emmajane went, too, and were made much of by the ladies of Lawrence. The preacher came to bury the baby properly and said he admired the name he had been given at his baptism very much indeed.

Now Lije met many people in Lawrence—from fiery abolitionist newspaper editors to men like big, dark, wild-haired Jim Love, black-bearded James Montgomery, and the elegant dandy, Dr. Jennison. They all seemed to know his pa and called him by name.

Once Jim Montgomery used a word Lije had not heard before, "Jayhawker." When he was alone with his pa, Lije asked, "Pa, what does that word mean?"

Tulley laughed. "That's what you and me and Jake Cousins are, Lijah. It means an abolitionist raider. It's opposite of the Missourians, the bushwhackers. All we got in common with them is that we're both night riders."

While the entire country held its breath, pondering the coming election in November and the threat of civil war, Kansas Territory baked in a summer of unrelieved drought. The dust burned hot as lava. Cracks opened in the soil. Fish could be caught by hand in the drying-up ponds. Hot winds killed the plants and seared the corn in the field before the tassels could develop. The water level in the Tulley well dropped and dropped. Ab and Lije had to slaughter the spring-born pigs because they had no feed for them. There were no crops to harvest, no blackberries or plums or grapes. Lije and Ab caught fish and turtles from the ponds and hunted for any game they could find and carry home—thin deer, prairie hens just feathers and bones. The family lived on this, and on corn bread made from last year's meal, hominy, and hickory nuts. They all grew thinner, but, Lord be praised, no Tulley sickened.

Alice Tulley and the girls sometimes stood at the window to watch the heat lightning flashing on the horizon. They prayed for rain, but none came. The Tulleys said tearful good-byes to neighbors who had come hopefully to Kansas Territory for good land and who were now leaving, driven out by the cruel climate. In August hail came pelting down out of a green sky, but it was too late to save what people had tried hard to grow. Even if the corn plants had lived, hailstones the size of black walnuts would have beaten them to nothingness. Jake Cousins took his wagon up to Iowa and brought back corn and wheat flour that he shared with the Tulleys. The food, he explained, had cost him nothing. It was a gift from abolitionists in the East who wanted to show their appreciation to the Kansas Jayhawkers.

"We ain't leaving this territory," Lije heard his pa vow from the cabin door after Cousins had unloaded the bags of food. "We'll hang on here to do the work we come for—what John Brown would want us to do. Mebbe we'll half starve, but we'll go to Missouri soon as the fall comes. We won't forget John Brown and what he died for."

"Nobody's going to forget him," said Cousins with a laugh. "There's even a song about him now. I heard it in Iowa. Everybody's singing it. It's got a real catchy tune." In a good, deep baritone voice, Jake Cousins sang:

> John Brown's body lies a-moldering in the grave,
> But his soul goes marching on.
> Glory, glory, hallelujah,
> His soul goes marching on!

"Oh, my God!" breathed Alice Tulley, standing next to Lije. "That won't let folks forget him and what he done."

Ab asked, "And everybody you know in Iowa's singing it? Alice, get a pencil and paper and we'll write it down. Sing it again, Jake. It's a powerful thing, that song."

Cousins said proudly, "Folks are singing it all over the North. Mebbe we ought to sing it over in Missouri."

"Not there, but they'll be hearing from you and me and my boy, Lijah, over there real soon." Ab's hand fell heavily onto Lije's shoulder. "It's time for Lijah to go. A good man who promised me he'd ride with us just left last week for Nebraska. He couldn't stand it here no more. We need another man, and Lijah will have to fill in for him. He's a mite too young, and it'll be dangerous, but we need somebody and he wants to go."

Going to Missouri? Going soon? Elijah's heart did cartwheels in his chest. He scarcely heard Cousins saying something about the upcoming election until he heard his pa cry out, "I wish I could vote for this here Lincoln in a national election, but men in territories can't vote. The slave hounds will be able to vote because Missouri's a state. But not us. If Mr. Lincoln gets elected, it won't be because we helped him get in, and that's a pity."

Cousins said, "Ab, there's plenty of men in the North who favor him. There are other men running, three of them, but in Iowa they say Lincoln will win."

"I pray so," said Alice Tulley.

"So does all of Lawrence," agreed Cousins with a nod.

Autumn came and with it, rain. Lije and his pa, glad to see it, went out into their brown, dead cornfield just to stand in the downpour and feel the cool wonder. The rain came too late to save the crops, but it revived the animals and refilled their well, and for that they were grateful.

In mid-September, Ab Tulley and Jake Cousins set a date for their raid. They chose a night of the new moon. That could give some light to see by, but not too much. A lone rider, a Jayhawker, had come from Missouri two days before to tell Cousins where two runaway slaves would be waiting in a thicket just over the river. If someone would come for them from Kansas, they'd wait there five days. They had food for only that much time, and they dared not move from the thicket to try to find more. If they were caught, they would be returned to their master, beaten, and probably sold to new owners deeper in the South.

Jake Cousins arrived at dusk in the wagon they would be taking. Ab and Lije Tulley were ready for him with pistols, rifles, and saddle horses. Blankets and food for the slaves, Lije knew, were already in the wagon.

Alice Tulley saw her husband and son off. Grim-faced, she embraced and kissed them both, then whispered to each in turn, "May God ride with you."

The Tulleys rode on each side of Cousins' wagon in silence. Lije heard only the calls of night birds, the sound of the horses' hooves on falling leaves, the booming of frogs in ponds, and the creak of the wagon. They crossed low-water creeks at fords the men knew, and then they came to a landing on the banks of the Missouri River.

Ab Tulley sounded a strange, two-note whistle, and a voice came out of the darkness below them. "Who'd you be?"

"Friends from Kansas. Friends of Mr. Hawkins. He sends us."

"Then come on, friends. I know Mr. Nelson Hawkins."

Lije's breath caught in his throat. Hawkins—that was one of the names John Brown had used when he was in Kansas.

Ab Tulley spoke now, "We'll be taking the ferry now, son. Our friends are waiting for us. There's a landing here just below us. Rein Banner in behind my horse. He'll follow her aboard. Jake'll go first."

Lije did as he was told. In the dim light of the moon he spied the ferry, a side-wheel steamboat.

He heard the wagon rattle down and aboard. Then his pa followed and after him, Banner. Almost at once, the ferry began its quiet glide over the slow-moving river. No one dismounted. No one spoke. Lije strained his hearing. There was a little splashing of the wheels beneath him, but that was all. Their arrival on the other side of the river was done so smoothly and expertly that there was nothing more than a crunch.

As they left the ferry, a male voice said, "Good luck to you. We'll wait, but don't take long. There's other riders out tonight on both sides of the river."

"Thank you kindly," said Absalom.

Missouri! Lije's heart was in his throat. This was forbidden ground, accursed ground. At his side, his pa whispered to him, "We ride right down the bank. Keep quiet. Do what I tell you to do."

The men and the wagon turned right into a forest of tall, black shapes down a narrow road. They went on for what seemed like hours to Lije, but in truth wasn't more than twenty minutes. Suddenly Tulley cried out like an owl. He sounded so much like one that if the startled Lije hadn't been right next to him, the boy would have thought it was a bird. Ab hooted twice, waited, then hooted three times, then two again.

There was no response from the tall thicket next to them. Once more his father hooted and listened. Nothing happened. Now Jake Cousins turned his mule-drawn wagon around and started back down the road ahead of the Tulleys. Lije wanted to speak to his pa, but dared not.

At the landing, the voice that had said, "Good luck," asked, "Got them, friends?"

"No," came from Ab Tulley. "The slave hounds must have tracked them, or they moved off themselves to somewheres else."

"They most likely got them back," growled the ferryman. "I saw torches and heard dogs baying downstream last night. Friends, I'll take you back now. You can't be lucky every time. Yours ain't a certain business."

"No, it ain't," agreed Absalom. Once aboard the ferry, traveling back over the river to safety, he asked Lije, "How do you take to raiding for slaves?"

"I was scared, Pa."

"Sure you were scared. You'd be a tomfool if you weren't, and this ain't a trade for fools. You done well, son."

"What if Missourians had showed up?"

"We'd shoot at them and them at us."

"It's like a war then, Pa?"

"Almost, but I reckon it's worse because it's got to be so secret and there's no medals in it."

"What if there's more Missouri men than us some time and they catch us raiding? What'll they do to us?"

Jake Cousins answered for Ab. "Tie us to trees and

shoot or hang us —the same thing us Jayhawkers would do to them if we caught them in Kansas."

"Do soldiers do that?"

"No, they behave better. I was in the Army during the Mexican War, and I can tell you what soldiers do. They got rules to follow. Us and slave hounds don't."

"When'll we go out again?" asked Lije.

"You're a real fire-eater, ain'tcha?" said Cousins. "We'll go when we get news that we can trust that there's slaves waiting somewheres for us. Mebbe later on us Jayhawkers will go with a big band of Kansas riders and attack a slave hound's farm and take his black people, but that time hasn't come yet. We're just getting together, forming into part-time soldiers, the kind folks call militia, all over this territory. We . . ."

Ab interrupted. "And so are the bushwhackers. They ain't just milking their cows two times a day. They're gathering, too. Meantime we do what we always do, just us two neighbor men keeping the faith with old John Brown. I don't know that him and his sons always came back with a full wagon load every time neither. We'll have better luck next time, God willing!"

Chapter Four

THE NEXT TIME
TO MISSOURI

*I*n mid-October, a message came to Jake Cousins that there were five slaves—three men, a woman, and a child—wanting an "escort" away from a farm some ten miles east of the Missouri River. According to Jake, they were waiting at the Prentiss plantation. He said, "I heard of this farm. It's a big one. This Prentiss is a big landowner and of the bushwhacker persuasion to boot. He's said to be a hard case who works his black people hard. No wonder they want to get away from him."

Ab Tulley spoke quietly. "Then we'll go over and get them. When, Jake?"

"Tomorrow night when the moon's half full. I'll take my wagon. Will you take yours?"

"No, I'll have to ride in yours with you, Jake. One a my team's gone lame. My boy here'll come with us on his bay. Where are the slaves supposed to be—in another thicket like last time?"

"No, in the smokehouse where they can lock themselves in until we come at night with the secret knock. Prentiss is a rich man. One a the slaves who wants to get away is a carpenter. He'd be worth hundreds of dollars if he was to be sold. The woman's a cook. She's worth money, too." He laughed now. "Prentiss sure won't want to lose them two."

Lije listened impatiently to this, then asked excitedly, "Mr. Cousins, who fetches you the messages? Is it always the same rider?"

Cousins smiled. "No, it ain't always the same rider. Sometimes the message comes by wagon or by horseback. Sometimes it's just some words whispered to me in Lawrence. Sometimes it's just a map or a note. But whatever man or woman brings me the message has got to have the passwords to go along with it."

Lije shook his head. A woman on the Underground Railroad? He asked, "What are the passwords?"

Tulley broke in laughing. "Tell him, Jake. If he's old

enough to go over there with us, he's old enough to know."

"All right. The Jayhawker who comes from Kansas says his last name's either Nelson or Hawkins. He can also say he's named Gideon—Mister or Missus or Miss, that is. Gideon was John Brown's favorite Bible hero."

Lije asked, "Do they sing 'John Brown's Body,' too?"

Cousins shook his head, smiling. "That song ain't well known over the river. It's our war cry, Elijah. All the North is singing it. It's a song to be marching by, and men will, too."

"Yes, it'll be a tune to go to war with," promised Ab Tulley.

The next night the three of them went out in a fog that hugged the ground. A ghostly light from the half moon shone down on trunks and tops of trees, making Lije feel himself in another world, a dreamlike place that lulled his spirits and calmed his excited nerves. As they crossed the river on the ferry once again, the boy's heart started to beat more swiftly. Trying to quiet the snorting, head-tossing Banner, who didn't take to the smell of the water, Lije looked out over the river. Fog lay like smoke over its surface.

There was some soft talk during the crossing this time, and by questioning the ferryman, Lije gleaned a little more information about the workings of the Underground Railroad all over the country. He'd known something about it, but had no idea it was so wide-spread and so well organized. Slaves were being spirited north to freedom from all over the southern states, particularly those on the border. They were rescued and transported from station to station on the invisible railroad that ran all the way from Texas and Louisiana up to Canada. Once in Canada, slaves could not be caught and returned to their masters, but if they were caught in the northern states, they could be returned.

The ferryman seemed to like to talk to fellow abolitionists. He told Lije of the places where slaves were hidden once they reached the North—in secret rooms built into houses, in trapdoor cellars, under bales of hay in barns, in attics over stores. People hiding a runaway slave, even in the North, had to be mighty careful, though. If they were discovered, they would be punished by the law, while the slave would be dragged away.

Cousins said, "We move ours fast as we can. A person can't hide for long in a cabin or a little patch of woods. But we ain't too far from the Nebraska line here, so the next station ain't too far off." He sighed. "All the same, it takes me a whole night getting to it. All I know is that one place, and my good friends here don't even know that. Somebody else takes the slaves to the next station, and that's all that one Jayhawker knows about. It's a good system, but it ain't good for a person's nerves."

The Missouri side of the river was covered by a milklike white haze with the dark shapes of trees rising through it.

Lije heard Cousins' final words to the ferryman. "Yep, it's a good night for our kind of work. Don't you fret. I got a good map and know the way. Has there been any commotion on the riverbank tonight?"

"Not one blessed sound. Not even any owl hooting."

Lije heard Cousins and his pa chuckling.

"Wait for us here," ordered Jake.

"I will. I won't answer no horn calls from anybody else, and they can't see my boat in the fog. Good luck to you."

"Thank you, friend," said Jake Cousins.

Then the wagon went up onto dry ground, and Lije led Banner off the bobbing craft. As he mounted the horse and gathered up the reins, he felt Banner shuddering under him. Banner danced sideways a few steps, catching Lije's nervousness. But the boy's soft crooning and caressing of his neck calmed the horse down, and he set off at a trot behind the wagon. Banner and the wagon made little noise on the wet leaves covering the narrow road. No one spoke. The only sounds came from the cold night winds.

Their route took them through hilly, heavily wooded country. There were birdcalls and the sounds of some invisible animals moving about at the side of the road, but nothing came out on their path to challenge them, and Lije was glad. With every step Banner took, Lije's fright deepened. He tried hard to focus his thoughts on the fearless John Brown, but they kept straying, moving irresistibly to worry over this mission. He grew more and more nervous with every mile they traveled.

Finally Jake Cousins reined his mules to a halt and started down another road, this time one leading north. They traveled under overhanging branches for a time and then past cleared fields. The fields meant they were approaching the Prentiss plantation.

Cousins halted, and he and Ab Tulley got down from the wagon. Lije, his big hat pushed down over his ears for warmth, rode up to take the mules' reins from his neighbor's hand. His job was to hold the wagon in readiness for its passengers. He could see a cabin ahead, a small, dark shape not far from the much larger two-story building that had to be the Prentiss house. Lije watched the two Kansas men move forward, picking their way over the ground to the smokehouse cabin. It had been marked on Cousins' map, Lije knew.

Would there be a dog to run up and bark a warning? Would Pa shoot it or hit it with his pistol? That would make noise, too, plenty of it. Slave saving was a risky trade!

And then it came, a man's deep shout from the veranda of the house. "I see you, you sneaking Kansas Jayhawkers. I see you on my land! You ain't getting my slaves tonight or any other night. I've got a bead drawed on one of you, and my son here's got one on the other one."

Lije strangled a cry of horror. Pa and Jake had walked into a trap, caught in the open. What would they do?

Jake Cousins answered for them all with his pistols, shooting into the blackness of the deep veranda. An instant later, red flashes spurted from the guns in Ab Tulley's hands.

Then came the firing from the Missourians.

Lije saw his father crumple to the ground. Then Cousins fell, clutching his stomach. Horrified, Lije dropped the mules' reins, turned Banner around, and made ready to gallop away. This is what Pa had told him to do if he was ever killed on a raid. Get away and get away fast!

"You, the one on the horse. Stop!" came a bellow only feet away from Lije.

A dark form hurtled out of tall bushes, leaped for Banner's bridle, caught it and stopped him. Though the horse reared, his hooves flailing the air, the man hung on. The minute the horse came down, the figure clawed Lije from the saddle before the boy could get his pistol from his belt. He hurled Lije to the earth, put a heavy foot on his back and thundered, "Lay there, Jayhawker. Don't you move one bit." It was the same voice he'd heard calling threats from the veranda.

Half stunned by his fall, Lije lay on his belly, his face in the damp soil. He heard the thud of running footsteps, heavy ones, and could now see three pairs of boots. Aching with terror, he listened to the conversation above his head.

The first voice he'd heard said, "Gabe's fetching a lamp from the house so we can get a look at this one here. I looked at the other two already. They're dead. They won't be coming here again to steal what ain't theirs. Ain't it a fine thing Gabe overheard that sassy cook of mine reminding her brat to go to the smokehouse and wait for the Kansas men? She didn't know Gabe was anywheres in earshot. We got the truth out of her real easy, and she's locked up in her quarters with them others." The man chuckled and added, "Hey, here's my boy Gabe with the lamp now. You done right fine, sons, just what I told you to do. Now let's get this Jayhawker to his feet and see if we want to hang or shoot him, too."

Gasping, Lije was hauled up by someone very strong and his pistol jerked from his belt. He was left to dangle from a very tall man's arms. A coal oil lamp was shoved into his face, blinding him, while the Missourians inspected him.

He couldn't think. He couldn't move. His mind wouldn't work at all. He stared at them as they stared at him. Except for the eldest one, they were young, dark-haired, clean-shaven men. The oldest was shorter and fatter, with dark hair and a full, reddish beard streaked with black and gray. This had to be Prentiss.

The man said angrily, "Even with his hat on, I can tell this is a boy who ain't put a razor to his chin one time. Who'd you be, you Kansas brat?"

"Hawkins, Nelson Hawkins," stammered Lije, using the only name he could think of other than his own.

"Who're those men?"

Lije stuttered, "My pa and a neighbor of ours."

"Abolition men?"

"Yes, sir, they were." Tears of grief over his pa and shame at his capture filled Lije's eyes.

Prentiss was scornful. "Jayhawkers are robbing the cradle now, ain't they? Well, I won't shoot you, young Hawkins. I won't hang you either. But I am going to see to it that you get the whipping you deserve. Then I'm going to send you back home with the men you came with. It'll save us the trouble of burying them. Dan, you and Gabe throw the dead men into the wagon. I'll take this horse. It looks to me to be a good one, better than a dirty thief of a Jayhawker deserves. I bet he stole it in Missouri. Matthew, you give Hawkins here a hiding he'll remember all his life."

"How do you want it done, Pa?" Matthew's voice was deeper than his father's. "With a horse whip or a rope?"

"No, over your knee, the way you learn little brats to keep their noses out of other folks' lives. That'll teach him to stay home in Kansas."

Lije was thrown down, lifted up, and had the back of his trousers hauled down. Then he was forced over the young man's uplifted knee, and his hat was jerked down over his nose. Matthew Prentiss slapped with his right hand. On and on went the pummeling, alternating with punches. Harder and harder. Never had Lije had such a whipping. As the beating continued, pain engulfed his mind. He could only gasp in lungfuls of air between cries of anguish. He couldn't stop his wails, no matter how hard he tried. The agony in his soul at his pa's death and the pain of the beating made him wish he had died with him.

Finally it was over, and his hat was jerked up so he could see. He was lifted up and hauled to the wagon. Catching hold of the seat so he would not collapse, Lije shifted a foot and a terrorized mule stepped on it. Fresh pain assailed Lije, a pain so intense he could only groan. He was flung up onto the seat. The reins were thrust into his hands and the mules' rumps were struck hard by strong hands.

The animals took off at a bone-jarring pace that became a gallop as shouting and rock pitching followed them. Unable to sit because of the stinging pain in his buttocks, Lije stood up in the wagon, howling at the mules, sawing at the reins till he calmed them to jerky trotting down the road they'd traveled on so hopefully, so boldly such a short time ago. A glance over his shoulder showed Lije the bodies of his father and Jake

Cousins, bouncing about as the wagon jolted. The sight of them brought fresh tears to his eyes. He slowed the mules to a walk out of respect for the men. They shouldn't be jolted so. He sobbed as he drove, after easing himself painfully onto the seat.

Almost mindlessly Lije made the turning and followed the road to the river. The fog had grown even thicker there. He whistled in Ab Tulley's two-note signal and heard the familiar voice out of the swirling whiteness. "You got a wagon load?"

"Yes, sir. My pa and his friend."

He could see the man at the ferry now as he came nearer. The ferryman asked, "What do you mean?"

"Those Missourians were waiting for us. They're dead. They killed Pa and Mr. Cousins and beat me up."

"No, no! I'm sure sorry, lad." The ferryman was silent, then asked, "Did you tell them your name?"

"I said I was Nelson Hawkins."

"Good. Did you tell them how you got over the river?"

"They didn't ask me. Mebbe they forgot to. Please take me across now. I can't talk no more, mister. I can't take no more."

"Once you're on the other side, can you make it home by yourself, son?"

"Yes, sir. I can do that. Pa would expect me to."

*   *   *

Unable to walk because of the terrible whipping and the pain in his toes, Lije stayed abed, lying on his stomach thinking and grieving while his ma and Mrs. Cousins prepared for the funerals of their men. Ira Cousins rode to Lawrence and returned with a preacher and two store-bought wooden coffins. The women lined them with blankets while the preacher and Ira dug graves in a little stand of walnut trees between their two properties.

Leaning heavily on Ira's arm, Lije managed to limp to the nearby grove. A heavy rain poured down throughout the short funeral service, which was attended by a number of folks who had come from Lawrence to honor the Cousins and Tulley families.

At the end of the service, Lije heard his mother say, "It's as if God Himself is crying tears over this today."

"Maybe John Brown's doing it," put in Clarissa.

Lije turned on her. "Stop that. That won't help us. We got to look ahead. It's just a rainy day, that's all. What do you expect during the fall? Now we got to think about going on with what we all got to do to stay on here. I'm most up to thirteen, and I can do a man's work, Pa's work, every kind'a work he did."

"Amen to that," agreed the Lawrence preacher. "I bet you can, son." He touched Lije's shoulder.

Side by side with his ma, Lije stood drenched, accepting the words of the Lawrence men and women as they approached and murmured words that were meant to comfort him. They didn't soothe him much. Pa was gone and so was John Brown, but their work wasn't done by a long shot, was it?

Chapter Five

HAPPENINGS

*T*hat November Abraham Lincoln was elected President. Riders galloped from Lawrence, spreading the welcome word to the Tulleys, Cousinses, and other Kansas farmers. There wasn't true rejoicing for the two families because of the very recent deaths, but the knowledge that the nation was getting a President opposed to slavery comforted them in their sorrow. Clarissa and Emmajane walked solemnly to the graveyard to tell their father the good news, while Lije sat by the fire soaking his aching foot in a bucket of water, waiting for the toes to heal.

Mrs. Cousins decided she and Ira couldn't keep up the farm. Ira wasn't big enough to plow and do the other things a strong man was needed for, and they didn't have the money to hire men to work it for them. Besides, workers weren't available. Men couldn't work all day and ride by night, and that was mostly what was going on in eastern Kansas now. Night after night the Tulleys heard the sound of hoofbeats on the road not far from their cabin, but never saw the riders. No one came to them. Lije figured the riders were Montgomery's or Jennison's men, Jayhawkers going to Missouri, but could not be sure. But if they were pro-slavery bushwhackers, they didn't come calling as they had when John Brown had gone out to free black people with Ab Tulley as his partner.

The Cousinses couldn't find a buyer for their land, so they had to abandon it. They went to live in Lawrence with Mrs. Cousins' bachelor brother, a barber.

The end of December, Ira came to visit and told the Tulleys of a raid some Kansas Jayhawkers had made on the plantation of a rich Missouri slave owner named Walker. Warned that a Jayhawker named Montgomery was coming with many riders, the Walkers were ready for them, just as the Prentisses had been for Ab Tulley and Jake Cousins. The Kansans were Quakers, not armed riders, and they rode up openly and asked the Walkers for thirty slaves. The Walkers fired on them, killing one Quaker and wounding another. The wounded man and a companion hid for two days, but eventually they were rooted out and killed with shotguns.

Lije shuddered. How like his pa's failed venture this was! He asked, "Who warned the slave hounds that Kansas men were coming?"

Ira knew his name. "He calls himself Charley Hart. At least that's the name he used when he hung around Lawrence. Somebody said his real name's William Quantrill. He don't come to Kansas anymore. Anyhow, he told on the Quaker men. He got paid for doing it, I bet."

Alice Tulley shook her head in horror. "Killing Quakers? God in heaven! Quakers never lift a finger to harm anyone, not even to defend themselves. It's against their faith." She sighed, threw a shawl over her shoulders, and went to the barn to see the chestnut horse, which was lame again.

From atop his horse, Ira asked, "Lije, will you be going out with the Jayhawkers when spring comes?"

"I don't know. I hear hoofbeats on the road going past the cabin, but I never see any riders. And nobody comes asking me to be his partner. Maybe they think I ain't old enough." He changed the subject. "How's Lawrence treatin' you?"

"Pretty fair. The schoolmarm's nicer than the one here. My uncle's all right to live with, but Ma cries a lot over Pa."

Lije nodded. "So does mine—in the night when she thinks nobody can hear her. But I do."

Ira gazed up at the gray sky that promised snow. "I better be getting back. The folks there say that war's coming for sure. Mebbe it'll last long enough for us to fight in it. So long, Lije."

"So long, Ira."

Standing at the cabin door, favoring his sore foot, Lije thought sourly of what day it was—Christmas Eve. Neither he nor Ira had mentioned it or wished each other a merry Christmas. How could it be merry this year? There were no gifts to exchange and a great deal to grieve over.

The next news that came to the Tulley farm came the last day of January. Again Ira brought it. He rode up whooping, "Lije, Lije!" He told them that Kansas was no longer a territory, but a real state of the Union. It had come in on January 29 as a free soil—no slavery state.

Ira cried out, "Oh, you should have seen the fuss that went on in Lawrence. Men were racing up and down the street on horses, and yelling and firing pistols in the air. Ma wouldn't let me out for fear a my getting hit. I seen it from an upstairs window over the barber shop. I hear tell great big guns called cannons are being sent by the South into Missouri and by the North here into Kansas for when we go to war. Men from all around Lawrence are bringing their rifles and pistols and shotguns and joining up into a militia. Why don't you go to Lawrence and be a Jayhawker again, too? You're big enough. Ain't your toes all right by now?"

"Just about," said Lije. "Once I get the seed corn in the ground, I'll come. I want to go over the river again. I want to find a dark-headed man with a red beard with gray and black in it."

Mid-March 1861 came and went. Abe Lincoln took office as President, and Lije went to Lawrence. He had waited until the spring planting was over and the sow the Cousinses had left them as a gift had given them six piglets. Then, with his mother's reluctant permission, he rode his father's chestnut horse to town and found tall, bearded Mr. Montgomery. He told the man, "I'd be Elijah Tulley. My pa got killed over in Missouri last fall. He used to go on raids with John Brown. I come here to join you if you'll take me. I want to ride with you to the farm of a Missouri man by the name of Prentiss."

Montgomery shook Lije's hand as if he'd been a grown man and said, "We know all about you. You're Ab Tulley's boy. We made a little visit to the Prentiss place last month. We got his slaves. We went there for your pa's and Jake Cousins' sake. We had to kill three of the old man's sons—good fighters they were—but Prentiss got away. We chased him far as we could, but he had a real good horse, a red bay. Then we came back and burned down his buildings."

Lije nodded and sighed inwardly. Prentiss had ridden Banner to safety, of course. So he wouldn't be settling the score with the Prentisses himself, then. The Jayhawkers had done it for him, but it wasn't the same.

Lije told Montgomery, "The red bay was my horse. Prentiss stole him. I want him back."

"Maybe you can get him back. We'll send for you when we go out next time. A messenger will come to tell you where to meet us. When we ride out, there are a lot of us, almost an army. There's always safety in numbers. Go home now and wait. That's what most of us do. We go about our daily business but come out when we're called. Sometimes that makes it hard to get our daily business done properly."

"Yes, sir, I'll come, and I'll be looking for old man Prentiss when I do."

"You'd be expected to, given what's happened. How old are you?"

Lije lied. "Sixteen—almost."

Montgomery smiled, letting the boy know he wasn't believed. He said, "Well, we've got other big boys your size. You were over to Missouri before, so you know what to expect. We don't use our own names when we go, and we don't carry anything on us that can say who we are. Bushwhackers could come over and hurt our families. What do you want to be called?"

Lije answered without hesitating a moment. "Joshua. That's what John Brown said I ought to have been named."

"We've got a Joshua already. How about 'Red' because of your hair? I never saw hair that dark a red color before."

"Red'll do just fine, Mr. Montgomery. What're you called?"

"Sometimes Mr. Cross, sometimes other names."

A skinny, short-shanked boy came riding up to the Tulley cabin on a fat horse two days later. He asked for Red and whispered a message to Lije, then galloped off to the west as fast as if he were a Pony Express rider carrying the mails to California.

"You're going out tonight, ain'tcha?" asked Alice Tulley.

"That's right, Ma. There'll be a lot of us this time. The rider he sent said Mr. Montgomery's going, too."

"Oh, Lijah, I don't think I could stand to lose you, too." Tears filled his mother's eyes.

"You won't, Ma. Mr. Montgomery knows what he's doing."

She stared dully at Lije and said, "Your pa thought so, too, and so did those poor Quaker men who were betrayed by a man they trusted."

"I'm a Jayhawker, Ma," Lije told her. "I have to go out."

"I know you do. Pa would expect it." She turned away to the stove and banged the lids about.

Using wooded trails he knew, Lije arrived at dusk at the rendezvous Montgomery had set, a glade surrounded by tall oaks. Thirty or so men and boys his size sat their horses there, talking softly. Occasionally one of them dismounted and checked saddle girths and pistols.

James Montgomery rode up to Lije, gave him a loaded pistol and spare bullets, and said, "Ride around to every man now. Get his name and tell him you're called Red."

Lije did as he was told. He collected names and handshakes, then rode back to wait at the edge of the gathering crowd. He hadn't recognized a single rider, but then the Tulley farm was pretty isolated. These could be mostly Lawrence folks.

At Montgomery's sharp call, the Jayhawkers started off at a brisk trot, riding east. As they rode, no one spoke to Lije, but he could hear snatches of quiet conversations going on around him. The talk was all of the war that was to come, not of the night's mission. States in the South were threatening to secede from the Union, and the North would not permit that to happen without a fight. A number of the riders vowed they would join the U.S. Cavalry and fight like soldiers. Others said they'd see how matters turned out in Kansas first. They felt they could be more useful to the Union cause as Jayhawkers.

Their ride was long. They crossed the border into Missouri overland below a loop of the great river. They passed through woods, meadows, and plowed fields until they came to a house and outbuildings beside a creek.

Once they arrived, the Jayhawkers didn't try to be quiet. They yelled, "Come out with your hands up or we'll shoot into the house."

A fattish man in a long, white nightshirt emerged, followed by a woman and two small girls.

"Where are your slaves?" asked Montgomery.

At his shout, a young man and a boy came running out of a cabin. Both were blacks in ragged clothing.

Montgomery now ordered his men, "Take two of this Missourian's horses and put these people on them. You, Miller, and you, Joshua, get down. You know what to do."

A tall Jayhawker and a short one dismounted, ran past the Missourians into the house, and came out with a big jug of what Lije recognized as coal oil. Joshua splashed it over the porch and onto the walls, then tossed the bottle inside, where it crashed on the puncheon floor.

Miller lit a match and threw it into the house. It blazed up almost at once. The woman shrieked in terror.

"We'll go now!" thundered Montgomery, turning his horse about and leaving at a fast canter. Lije waited for a moment, shocked in spite of himself at what he saw. He and another lad near him sat on their horses, stunned at the sight. Then Joshua, mounted now, caught the other boy's bridle, cursed him, and forced his mount to move alongside his own horse. An instant later, Lije had reined the chestnut away.

Joshua roared at the boy, "Let's get out of here before some bushwhackers see the fire and come riding. Make tracks for the border!"

The Jayhawkers got the slaves over the line into Kansas without incident. The raid was over and successful. Once in Kansas, Montgomery congratulated each man. He slapped Lije on the shoulder as he rode past him. The slaves followed an elderly-looking man, who rode a dapple gray down a side trail, while most of the other riders headed toward Lawrence. Some split off wordlessly to make their separate ways home. That was what Lije did, and as he rode, he thought dully of the raid. He'd taken no joy in it—none at all. The firing of the house had sickened him.

As he neared his own cabin, Lije smelled smoke. A forest fire? The cornfield ablaze? He put the chestnut to a gallop. As he came to where the cabin should have been, he saw nothing but black ashes and rising plumes of pale smoke, as gray as the dawn. The barn, corncrib, and springhouse still flickered red with little tongues of flame.

"Ma, Clarissa, Emmajane!" he shouted as the horse danced sideways, afraid of the fire. "Where are you?"

"We're here, Lijah," came his mother's cry as she ran toward him from the graveyard grove, her arms outstretched. Her daughters followed. They came stumbling to his horse, where the girls caught hold of one of the stirrups, sobbing.

Alice Tulley lifted her tear-stained face to tell Lije, "Thank goodness, you're safe. Bushwhackers did this. They came just after you rode out. They were the same men who came the night John Brown was here. Judah Hamilton and the rest. They asked for your pa by name, and when I said Missourians had killed him last year, they called me a liar. They said he rode out tonight with Montgomery. They said they'd heard there was a Tulley with him. I showed them your pa's grave, but they said it was a Jayhawker trick and nobody was buried there. They shot and killed our old Watchie and set fire to the house and everything else. We lost everything we owned except for the money I hid inside my dress when I heard all their horses coming to the cabin."

Lije said tonelessly, looking at the smoke, "We saved two slaves and we burned out a Missouri family tonight, Ma. Don't the Bible say 'an eye for an eye—a tooth for a tooth'?"

"It does, son. That's what it says."

"What'll we do?" sobbed Clarissa.

"I don't know," said Lije.

"We can't rebuild," came from Mrs. Tulley. "I haven't got the strength, son. And we can't sell. If the Cousinses couldn't, we can't neither."

"Ma, I know we can't do that." Lije nodded. He motioned to the desolation around them. "I say we got to do what Mrs. Cousins did. Leave."

"Leave Pa? He's buried here!" cried Emmajane.

"Yes, I know, but he can't help us now. I reckon this is what he'd expect us to do. He'd say to keep alive. We'll starve come winter if we don't leave. I see they fired the cornfield, too, and the smokehouse. Did they burn the wagon and take away all our animals?"

Mrs. Tulley said angrily, "They shot all the pigs, every one, but one of the men said our team wasn't good enough to be run off. The horses are too old. They put 'em in the woods and left us the wagon and the harness Pa used to patch up all the time. They didn't plan to kill us—just drive us out."

"Then we'll go, Ma, and figure they did just that, but we ain't done with them."

"Where'll we go, back to Iowa?" asked Clarissa, rubbing her smoke-reddened eyes.

"No, we'll go to Lawrence. We got friends there.

I'm sure Ira's ma will take you in, and I'll go see Mr. Montgomery right off."

Suddenly Alice Tulley laughed. "They were polite to us, son. Would you believe the bushwhackers took off their hats to me before they rode off. They said we should have had the good sense to clear out of here earlier. Lije, you go bury Watchie now. Bury the pigs, too, while you're at it."

"Sure, Ma." A lump came into Lije's throat. He had loved their old dog. He'd known him ever since he could remember. Watchie had come with the family by wagon train from Iowa. He'd suffered here in Kansas, too. He'd lost an ear to frost, so he'd had a lop-eared look. It would be painful to bury Watchie. Lije wished he had a blanket to put around him, but he didn't.

As if she'd read Lije's thoughts, his mother took off her smoke-blackened apron and handed it to him. "For Watchie" was all she said.

Chapter Six

A STRANGE
PROPOSITION

The Tulleys waited until full daylight. Then they walked about to find whatever had not been burned. It was not much. Lije harnessed the team to the wagon, and without a backward glance, the family set off for Lawrence.

Lije knew where the barber shop on Massachusetts Street was located. He tied the team to a hitching post, went up the outside stairs to the second floor, and knocked on the door.

Mrs. Cousins was ironing. She came to the door,

flatiron in hand, took one look at Lije, and cried, "What's wrong, Elijah?"

"Bushwhackers burned us out last night. Ma and the girls are down below in the wagon."

"You get them right on up here."

Lije did as he was bidden. Afterward he ate a big breakfast of corn bread, ham, and fried eggs, then sat at the table with Mrs. Cousins, Ira, and Ira's uncle, who had come upstairs from the shop.

After both of the women and both girls had wept, Mrs. Cousins started talking while her brother nodded. She said, "Alice, we're sure sorry you lost your home, too, but I'd say you come to the right place here! Have you got any money, or did the bushwhackers get that, too?"

"We got some money, Sarah Mae."

"Good. I've got some big ideas. I've looked around here carefully. Lawrence needs a hat store for ladies who're getting tired of home-sewed sunbonnets. I found a store for rent. It's got living quarters above it and behind. There's room for all of us. I don't intend to inconvenience my brother much longer. You sew just fine. I seen your work. You and I can trim hats and sell them."

Lije's mouth opened and closed at the energy of the women. Mrs. Cousins' brother shook his head and said, "Ain't she a daisy, though? She always was."

Mrs. Cousins continued. "Alice, after you get some rest, we can go see about the store. I've got some money, too, plus blankets and pots and pans and things we took from our farm. You and me can wear my dresses. We're of a size. We'll make do, and before you can say Jack Robinson, we'll be trimming and selling bonnets. I know where to get hold of ribbon and straw and laces and feathers. No matter if the war does come, we can sell hats and things like reticules, too."

"Oh, Sarah Mae, you are a wonder," sighed Alice Tulley. "I just don't know. I thought Lije would get a job and I'd mebbe go to work as a housekeeper."

"Well, two little girls and a big chunk of a hungry boy won't make you look so good as a single woman would," said Mrs. Cousins scornfully.

Lije put in suddenly, "I won't be in the way of anybody. I plan to go see the Jayhawkers and ask them what to do."

The barber, Lucas Walker, put in, "That's a good idea, boy. I'd say you could go ride for the Pony Express farther west, but I think you're bigger than they want. They need boys that're smaller and lighter and short-legged so they don't burden a fast horse."

Lije took a sip of coffee. "I don't aim to leave Kansas, mister."

The barber nodded, unsmiling. "Not unless it's to go to Missouri, huh?"

"That's right. There's some men over there I want to see."

Clarissa piped up, "A Mr. Prentiss and Mr. Hamilton."

The barber leaned over to whisper to Lije, "While you're at it, you might look for a man called Quantrill."

Lije told him coolly, "I heard of him. He's the one that betrayed them poor Quakers and got them killed."

Ira said, "He surely is."

Mrs. Cousins and his mother continued to talk, making their plans. But Lije barely listened now. After all that had happened last night, he felt sleepy and weary. He also kept thinking of the Missouri family he'd helped burn out. Where had they gone? Had neighbors taken them in? He'd like to sleep some, but there was a burr at the back of his mind that had been there ever since his ma had told him one of the bushwhackers had said he knew there was a Tulley among the Jayhawkers. That meant just one thing to Lije—a spy among the Jayhawkers. Who could it be?

Lije got up, put on his hat, and said, "Thank you for the breakfast, Mrs. Cousins. I'm going to find Mr. Montgomery or Dr. Jennison. There's some business I got with them. Ma, you and the girls get some rest now."

Finding James Montgomery that day was easy. All Lije had to do was ask one of the loungers outside a saloon where he was. Everybody in Lawrence knew the famous Jayhawker and held him in deep respect. Montgomery was seated in a chair in the town's other barber shop having his beard trimmed. He greeted Lije with, "I didn't expect to see you so soon, Red."

"Mr. Montgomery, I didn't expect to come here so soon." Lije paused, then went on in a rush. "The fact is, us Tulleys got burned out last night by bushwhackers. They came over here while we were over there."

"Mmm," said the man. "We could have met them head-on. Too bad we didn't! I'm sorry about your place. Where are your folks?"

"I fetched us all here to Lawrence to stay with some good folks we know, the Jake Cousins family. The women are already making plans for living together here and selling bonnets. I don't want to be a burden on my ma. I got to find work."

Montgomery nodded as the barber snipped away. He said, "You're a fair hand with horses. I can get you work in a livery stable, and you can sleep in one of the rooms up over it. I take it you don't mind the smell of horses."

"I like it." Lije hesitated, then said softly, "I need to talk to you alone."

"Wait till I'm done here, and we'll go for a walk."

Lije waited, admiring the barber's skill with the scissors. He wouldn't grow a beard, he decided. But the day was coming fast when he'd have to start using a razor on his face. He wished his pa's hadn't burned in the fire. It had had a wooden handle, and wood can't stand up to flames.

Once James Montgomery was finished, he paid the barber and started down the newly built boardwalk with long-legged strides. "What do you want to tell me, son?"

"One of the bushwhackers told Ma that they burned us out because they heard a Tulley had gone out riding with Jayhawkers last night."

"He did!" Montgomery stopped to look down at Lije. "The devil he did!"

"Yes, sir. We think he thought it was my pa who rode with you. He didn't believe Ma when she showed him Pa's grave."

Montgomery ran his fingers through his beard as his gaze traveled down Lawrence's main street. He was silent for a while, then said, "I don't think we've got a spy in our midst, Red. My guess is that somebody who don't favor what we do saw you on your way to meet us and recognized that chestnut horse you rode. Wasn't that the one your pa used to ride?"

"Yes, sir, Flitch is."

"The bushwhackers could have found somebody on this side of the river to watch us and then ride to them with news. Not all Kansas folks are for abolition, you know."

"I know, Mr. Montgomery."

The man started walking once more and Lije fell in with him. "It appears to me that whoever told the bushwhackers on you knew your pa and knew his horse and mistook you for him. I reckon he didn't know Ab had been killed. That could be. I'm sorry this happened. It was bad luck, but I trust every man and boy in my band. Twenty-eight went over and twenty-eight came back, so nobody split off to tell the bushwhackers."

Now the man frowned and said quietly, "Things are heating up, and we're all getting ready for war. The more we know of what the other side is up to, the better off we'll be. You're a smart lad. I see that. I like the way you act and ride and talk. You don't lose your head."

Lije muttered, "Joshua had to pull me away from watching that fire over in Missouri last night."

Montgomery nodded. "That generally happens the first time a man sees somebody's home set afire or a man shot. That don't mean much. I been thinking you could be just the one we've been hoping would come along. Do you suppose you could do something special for us Kansas men that would help us out a lot?"

"If I can, I will."

"I figured you would. You appear to me to have a grown-up head on your shoulders. You've got your pa to avenge as well as the loss of your place. This is my proposition to you. Will you go over to Missouri and pass yourself off as a bushwhacker?"

"What?" Lije was astonished.

"That's right, pretend to be a good Missouri bush-whacker. Live with them. Eat with them. Ride with them. And find out all you can about them. I won't lie to you. It'll be dangerous—mighty dangerous."

Excitement rose in Lije's breast, but all he said was, "I dunno that I could do that. It's a tall order."

Montgomery nodded again. "That's why a boy could get away with it. Nobody would expect a boy to be a spy. Well, Red, think on it. You don't have to make up your mind this very minute."

Lije shook his head. "Ma would be scared to death if she knew."

"She won't know. Nobody will know but me and the person you'll report to in the Big Sni River country. That's where you'll be most of the time. That's where the bushwhackers hole up. You'll relay messages about when they plan to come over here and what else they're up to. You'll need a good horse, a faster one than that chestnut. It's too slow, and besides, it could be rec-ognized somewhere again. There's a black gelding at the livery stable, name of Crow, that'll fit the bill. What do you say to that?"

"I'll think on it, Mr. Montgomery. What'll I tell Ma if I decide to do what you ask?"

"Tell her you're traveling around the state with some men buying horses to sell to the United States Army. That work would take you all over, and you'd be gone for months at a time."

"Could I mebbe come back here to Lawrence now and then to see Ma and the girls?"

"If you're real careful not to let the Missourians catch you. I don't know. We'll see. You'll have to get them to trust you, Red. That'll be the hardest thing at first. Nothing that I'm asking you to do is going to be easy. It could get you horsewhipped or even killed, but it could get you the everlasting gratitude of people here in Kansas, once all the troubles are over. You'll have to watch everything you do and say, and you'll have to seem to agree every time with what the bushwhackers think and tell you. Could you do that?"

"I don't know, sir. I'll think on it."

"You do that, Red. Take a while. Then come tell me what you've decided. It's a big responsibility for a man—for somebody years older than you are."

"I know that, Mr. Montgomery. I know it, and it scares me."

"It ought to. That's a sign of sharp wits. I like that. You tell Mr. Bass at the livery stable to put you to work right now."

Lije recognized Bass right away as one of last night's Jayhawkers. When Bass heard his story, he sent him to the little room over the carriages and told him to get some rest. Lije would start work tomorrow currying and exercising livery horses, mending carriage harnesses, caring for saddles, polishing horse brasses, and cleaning out the stables. For this he'd get the room, his meals at a nearby restaurant, and three dollars a month.

Lije went up to the room, took off his boots, and fell onto the hard cot without pausing to notice that the room had only a washstand, basin and bowl, and nails for hanging up clothing. He pulled a brown blanket that smelled of horse sweat up over his shoulders and fell asleep at once.

What dreams he had! Horses galloped through them. Torches blazed. Voices shouted and screamed. He saw his pa's face and Jake Cousins' and the laughing faces of the Prentisses.

Then he saw John Brown as he'd seen him last, reaching down from the seat of his wagon to shake first his pa's hand, then his ma's, and finally his own. The great abolitionist's bright gray eyes grew larger and larger until they filled the entire dreamscape.

Lije Tulley sat up with a start, not knowing where he was at first. His gaze swept the barren little room. Yes, Bass' stable room in Lawrence. He was in Lawrence now.

But when he closed his eyes, all he could see were John Brown's eyes, demanding, commanding him.

"I'm going to Missouri," Lije whispered to himself.

Chapter Seven

NETTIE GAINES

*L*ije kept his thoughts and his dreams to himself for three days while he went about learning the livery stable business from Mr. Bass and talking with town Jayhawkers who frequented the place. He carried water, combed and curried the horses, filled mangers, forked hay, and exercised mounts, plus anything else Bass told him to do.

In particular, he became acquainted with Mr. Montgomery's gelding, Crow, whom he might be riding to Missouri someday. Crow was as black as the bird for which he was named, except for a white blaze on his face and three white stockings. He was fast, and he neck-reined just dandy. He could be ridden by nudgings with a man's knees, so the rider's hands would be free for pistols. Crow wasn't only fleet, he was also a jumper. Falling off only two times so far, Lije had taken him over four fence stiles and some ditches. Crow was a nervous animal, though, quick to take to a gallop and flighty at strange noises. But his mouth was tender, so he could be reined in and calmed down. He wasn't Banner, but he was a good horse and Lije liked him.

In the evenings after he'd washed and then changed his clothing, Lije visited his family and the Cousinses.

It appeared to him that his mother and Mrs. Cousins were doing well in getting their business under way. They'd rented the shop, sewed muslin and calico curtains, brought in chairs and tables, and put up shelves. The sewing supplies they needed for the bonnets were ordered and would soon arrive. A bank had given them a small loan, and they'd each moved in over the shop. Clarissa and Emmajane were enrolled in a Lawrence school, and Ira was helping his uncle in his barber shop.

On the third night of visiting, after a piece of berry pie fresh from the oven, Lije leaned back in his chair and launched into the story that Mr. Montgomery had prepared for him. He said, "Mr. Bass will be sending me out west to help buy horses for the Army. He thinks I'm a good hand with them."

"You won't go alone, will you, son?" asked Mrs. Tulley.

"No, course not, Ma. There'll be some men along. It won't be dangerous." He didn't take to lying, but he had to keep the Jayhawkers' secret.

He waited. He'd known what she would ask and had been ready for it.

"Well, then, go on, Lijah."

He let go his tension. He'd tell Mr. Montgomery his decision first thing the next morning.

First thing in the morning, Lije sought out James Montgomery. He found him in company with Dr. Jennison, who led a band of abolitionist Kansans called the Redlegs because of the red-topped boots they wore. The two men were sitting on the front porch of Lawrence's best hotel, smoking cigars and seeming to enjoy the morning breezes. Relaxing there, they did not look like bold, dangerous men at all.

As usual, Jennison was dressed to the height of fashion in a tan frock coat, fawn-colored trousers, and highly polished Congress gaiters. As Lije approached them, he heard the doctor ask Montgomery, "Is this the lad you've been telling me about, James?"

"He sure is. We call him Red. Take off your hat, son, and let him see why."

Grinning, Lije removed his hat so the sun could turn his hair to the color of polished mahogany.

"Peculiar-colored hair, I'd say," came from Jennison after he flicked ash off his cigar. "No wonder you call him that. Where'd you get that shade of hair, boy?"

"From my ma. Hers used to be like this, but it's getting lighter and grayer now. It's had good cause to go gray."

"Yes." Jennison's face hardened. "I know your parents' story. I know Kansas. Men stand it better here than women do. Women have been known to go lie down among a flock of sheep because they got so lonesome. They can go mad here."

Lije nodded. "I heard tell of a woman who put a rope around her neck and hung herself from a tree 'cause the well on her farm went dry."

"It has happened," agreed Montgomery. "This is a hard land. Does your coming to see me mean you're going to take on the chore I asked?"

"Yes, sir, it does. I told Ma what you told me to, that I'd be away buying horses."

"That's a good enough story."

Montgomery stepped down from the porch and, coming up to Lije, he said very softly, "You'll be going to Missouri, but not just yet. When we send you, you'll be told what kind of developments over there we want to know about."

Lije asked, "When do you think I'll go?"

"Son, you keep working for Bass for now, but it's my guess that you'll be crossing over into Missouri for certain once some shooting starts on the East Coast. And that's expected any day now."

On the twelfth of April came the news that the whole nation had breathlessly awaited. Civil war had begun! South Carolina troops had fired on a federal installation, Fort Sumter.

Lije heard about it when Ira came sprinting up to him in the livery stable where he was currying a horse.

"Lije, the war's begun! It came over the telegraph wire to Fort Leavenworth and a rider brought it here." Ira's face was rosy with excitement. "My uncle says he's going to close his shop and join up in Lincoln's army when men get called for. You're big and tall. Why don't you say you're old enough and join up, too?"

Lije paused, holding the currycomb to his chest for a moment. Then he said, "Well, I ain't old enough, Ira. Besides, I can do my part by going around the state buying up horses and mules. Ma would have a fit if I tried to sign up when I wasn't old enough. You know that."

Ira looked crestfallen. "So would my ma. She wants me to go back to school."

"Go back. I wish I could."

Ira said, "I seen you talking with Mr. Montgomery and Doc Jennison the other day in front of the hotel. What'd you talk to them about?"

Lije grinned. "Jayhawking. What else?"

"Now that war's come, will they keep that up?"

"I don't see why not. Jayhawkers and bushwhackers ain't going to go away just because there'll be soldiers in Kansas and Missouri. The states are big enough for all of them. The Missourians won't be giving up their slaves to us like Christmas presents because of the war."

"No, I reckon not." Ira nodded. "Your ma will be glad you ain't going to try to run off and lie about how old you are and join the Army."

Not wanting to meet Ira's blue-eyed gaze, Lije went to the other side of the horse where he could not be seen. Ira had quick wits. He might be able to see by the look on Lije's face that he was lying and up to something, something his ma wouldn't take to at all.

That night Lije was summoned from his room by a boy Montgomery had hired to run messages. He was to come to the man's house right away.

To Lije's surprise, Montgomery was not alone when he came into the lamplit room filled with velvet-upholstered furniture. A tiny, gray-haired woman sat at a small marble-topped table across from the Jay-hawker. A long-stemmed glass was in her hand, and as she looked at Lije, she sipped red wine from it. She was dressed in a purple silk gown and had a beautiful paisley shawl over her shoulders. Who was she, and why was she here tonight of all nights?

James Montgomery addressed Lije. "Well, the war

has started. I think it's time for you to go. Red, this is Mrs. Nettie Gaines. Nettie, this boy is to be known as Red Quentin. He has told me that Quentin is his real middle name. If he's pressed to it, he can say his real first name's Joshua, can't you, son? That was the name John Brown said you should have."

"Yes, sir, that's what Mr. Brown said. It's out of the Bible."

"Excellent," agreed the woman in a soft voice.

"Take a seat, son." Leaning back in his own chair, Montgomery explained. "Nettie's going to take you to Missouri. She's an old friend and can be trusted. She's got iron nerves. She'll take you to find the men we want. Nettie, please tell Red what you plan to say to Quantrill, if you should meet him, or to any other bushwhackers."

The woman's voice was soft, but so hissing cold it made Lije shiver. "I plan to take an old horse and wagon, plus you and your horse, my boy, and cross the border. I'll ask straight out for directions to where the bushwhackers are holed up." She paused, then went on after a sip of wine. "I plan to say I lived here in Kansas for twenty years, and that my husband and I spoke out in favor of slavery, though the only slave we owned died before we ever came here from Virginia. I shall say my husband died of lockjaw two years ago on our farm. I'll tell them that my only child, my daugh-

ter, went crazy when her husband left her for the Cal
ifornia gold fields in 1850 and never came back again."
The woman's pale eyes held Lije's fast in a hard gaze.
She asked, "Do you follow me, my lad?"

"Yes'm. I do."

"Good, and do you want to know where you come
into this fine pack of lies?"

"Yes'm."

At this Montgomery chuckled.

Mrs. Gaines went on. "I plan to tell the bushwhackers that you are my daughter's only child and that I
can't keep you with me because you're so ornery and
are always up to mischief." She laughed. "I shall ask
them to take you in because there's no place for you
in Kansas since it's a free state now and you're strong
for slavery, like me. I'll tell them I'm going back home
to the East to live with my sister and that I'm selling
my farm here once I come back from delivering you
to the Missourians. To hide that Iowa accent of yours
I plan to say that you don't talk much because you
aren't long on brains, but you like horses and riding,
and you know how to handle firearms because your
grandpa taught you, figuring war would be coming
along soon and you'd make a soldier for the South. I'll
ask whatever bushwhacker we meet if he'll take you
into his band so the South can get some use out of
you since you're too young for the army."

All Lije Tulley could do was suck in his breath and then let out a long "ooh" that made the old woman grin at him.

She asked, "Would your mother recognize you from what I plan to say about you?"

"No, ma'am, she never would. I don't think anybody who knows me would. I did good enough in school, and nobody ever said I was dumb. They . . ."

"We know you aren't dumb," interrupted Montgomery. "We wouldn't send you over to Missouri if you were."

Lije asked, "Why send a lady at all, Mr. Montgomery? I could go alone."

"No. She'll be believed. You might not be if you just rode up saying you wanted to be a bushwhacker. Nettie isn't quite what she seems to be. She's been a stage actress for a long time—a mighty fine one, too."

The old woman nodded and smiled, then told Lije, "I've played a number of roles in Shakespeare's plays back East, queens mostly. I think I'll like the part I'm to play very much indeed. Don't worry, I shall get away with it, my boy. I hope you can. Your part will last longer and be far more dangerous. That's why I'll be most careful to say you don't talk very much. You won't be expected to, so you won't be so apt to let any wrong words slip out to make bushwhackers suspect you aren't what you claim to be."

She stood up and clapped her hands. "So when do we leave, sir?" she asked Montgomery.

"At dawn tomorrow morning, Nettie. The boy'll return here with his horse and blanket roll. Red, you're to take Crow."

"Yes, sir."

Mrs. Gaines nodded. "I'll be here with the wagon and horse you found for me. I certainly won't be traveling in style, it seems." She turned to Lije and asked, "Can you drive the mare like a good grandson should for his poor old grandma?"

"Yes, I can."

She came up to Lije now and touched his cheek. She smelled of rosewater. She said, "I once met John Brown in the East. I heard him speak to a crowd of people. I've not forgotten his words. I do this for him. I'm told this is why you're willing to act as a spy."

"That's the truth of it—that and my pa's getting killed, and other things."

"Yes, child, I've heard all about what happened to you and your family. These are bad times to be living in. I remember better ones in other years. To tell you the truth, I'm glad I'm not young anymore. Now I'll go upstairs to rest before I go out with such a fine-looking, redheaded boy at daybreak. I was in love with a red-haired boy a long, long time ago."

Montgomery told Lije, "Go back to the stable and get some sleep, too, if you can."

"Shouldn't I go tell my ma good-bye?"

"No. Bass will tell her you and some men left before dawn to buy horses they'd heard the Southern army wanted to buy, too, and that they had to get there first. There wasn't any time to waste. So you come here bright and early tomorrow without any fare-thee-wells to anybody. Now let me tell you the words that will let you know the people you can trust in Missouri. If somebody says 'Nelson' to you, you say 'Hawkins' in the next sentence you say. Then you can talk freely and know that you're with friends. You know those names?"

Lije smiled. "John Brown used them. I won't forget. Rest easy on that."

"Good luck to you, Elijah."

Chapter Eight

THE HOUSE WITH THE GRAY SHUTTERS

*I*t was still dark when Lije came down from his room to bridle and saddle Crow and tie his blanket roll behind the black gelding's saddle. Then he mounted, opened the stable door, and rode out into a gray dawn. Pink-and-gold streaks were showing in the eastern sky as he reached Montgomery's house. An old wagon with an old brown horse hitched to it was waiting in front of the picket fence.

Lije rode up to it, peered at the woman seated on it, and gaped in amazement. The elegant lady of the night before was gone entirely. An old, white-faced woman with wispy gray hairs sticking out beneath a faded blue calico sunbonnet glared at him as she pulled a tattered shawl over her widow's dress. All she needed was a corncob pipe in her mouth to look like somebody's great-great-grandma.

She told him, "Throw the saddle and blanket in the back, and tie the horse to the wagon. Then get up here, take the reins, and we'll get on our way. I've got money to pay for our ferries and lodgings, so don't concern yourself with that."

"Yes'm." Lije hastened to do what he was told, and soon they were heading out of Lawrence.

Lije didn't know the country below Lawrence well by daylight. He'd only seen it the one night he rode out with the Jayhawkers. But Mrs. Gaines, now old Granny Gaines, did. She surely wasn't taking the route Montgomery had. The wagon went over bad roads, jolting and jerking along in and out of ruts.

Lije had his doubts about the old horse, but she did well, and the woman told him, "Don't fret about the mare, my lad. She's like me. She's not so old and feeble as she looks. She's been doctored some, too. She'll get us to where you're going, then get me back to Lawrence again."

Lije asked, "How do you know Mr. Montgomery?"

She smiled. "My family knew his family long ago. I met him again back East when I met John Brown. Last week James saw a theater handbill that announced my troupe's upcoming performance in Topeka. He read my name, remembered me, and sent a letter offering me interesting work. That work is you."

Feeling very daring, Lije said, "This is so dangerous, he must be paying you plenty of money."

Mrs. Gaines sat up very straight. "Not one blessed red cent! He offered me money, but I wouldn't touch it. Has he offered you money?"

"No, ma'am, but I reckon he'll take care of my ma and sisters."

"He will see to it that your family are in no want while you're away. There'll be money, too, when you're done with your work. Soldier's pay. He says you're to consider yourself a member of the Kansas militia."

"Oh."

As he took the wagon along the Missouri River, catching glimpses of its blue waters through the thickets and trees, Lije pondered what lay ahead for him. What sorts of things did spies do?

After a while, he asked Mrs. Gaines, "Have you ever been a spy before?"

"No, not a real one. But I acted the part once in a play. A spy listens to what is said and remembers it even if it doesn't sound very important to him. He watches people in a way that doesn't make them suspicious of him. He tries to fit in wherever he is and not attract a lot of attention. Let me tell you how I'd act if I were you."

"I'd be pleased if you would."

"Be quiet most of the time, and don't stare at people. Always be polite. Never fight unless you have to. Don't write down anything that could be found on you. Don't argue. Do what your superiors tell you to do. Don't talk about yourself and your family."

"Ma'am, that's a lot of things not to do."

"Yes, it is, but I think you can do them, young Mr. Red. There's a basket in the back of the wagon. It's got cold corn bread and bacon in it. That's to be our breakfast and lunch."

They traveled all day, and by sunset they were still in Kansas, following the river. They were surely going a lot slower than the Jayhawkers had, Lije thought. During the day he had seen Mrs. Gaines consult a hand-drawn map and trace the route with her finger, then nod and put it back in her apron pocket. Afterward, she would tell him which way to rein the mare onto a road.

They'd rested the mare and themselves a few times, and once they'd stopped at a farmhouse and asked for cold spring water. Nevertheless they were weary by now.

The woman told Lije, "The road we're on should take us to the ferry that's supposed to be here at the river. We'll cross over before dark. There's supposed to be a tavern on the other side where we can stay

overnight. I was told it would be safe to stay there."
She laughed. "Missouri men don't like to hurt wom-
enfolks. They pride themselves on being courteous to
the weak and feeble."

Weak and feeble! Nettie Gaines? Lije shook his head.
There wasn't much weakness and feebleness about her
or his ma or Mrs. Cousins.

Luckily the ferry was waiting at the bank. The ferryman helped Lije get the wagon aboard and cast off.
With his helpers, he took the ferry across for the
twenty-five cents Mrs. Gaines gave him.

As they left, the ferryman told them, "You're my last
customers for the night. Last time I took people over
at night, I had a pistol to my head all the way and I
never got paid."

Mrs. Gaines asked calmly, "Jayhawkers or bushwhackers?"

"I don't know, ma'am. They wasn't Kansas Redlegs,
though. I could tell that by their boots. They didn't
tell me who they was, and I didn't ask. They might
have gone back by ferry elsewhere or never gone back
at all. There was twelve of them, all mounted on good
horses. They didn't talk at all while we got them over.
Now you and the boy be careful, ma'am. I wouldn't
want my ma out in no wagon at night."

"We'll take care. We got friends on this side of the
river. Thank you kindly."

The riverside tavern was only a large double cabin,

but there was hot food to be had, a bed for Mrs. Gaines and for Lije, and a place for the mare and Crow.

After a fried-chicken supper, Mrs. Gaines started up a conversation with the tavernkeeper, telling him the story she had planned out. When she finished, she asked if the man knew somebody who'd see to it that they got to the right Missouri men.

The tavernkeeper, a little, roundish man, told her, "Head north some. There's a house with gray-painted shutters a morning's ride from here. Stop and ask there. Maybe you'll find what you're looking for. Maybe not. They can tell you where to look further on if you don't. Can your boy ride and shoot?"

"Oh, Red surely can. That's about all he's good for, seems to me. He won't learn to read and write, though they tried to teach him. He's got the pistol his grandpa left him and the good horse I bought him before we left home."

The tavernkeeper's young wife nodded as she brought Lije and Mrs. Gaines more coffee. "Missouri could use more folks who think like your boy does. We figure there'll be fighting here pretty soon. He'd be a good soldier for the South, he's so big and strong."

Mrs. Gaines smiled at her. "That ain't what I have in mind for Red—to see him a soldier. I think, and he thinks, too, that he'd favor more riding with the likes of a Mr. Quantrill we hear so much about over in Kansas. I didn't spend good money getting my grandson a good horse for no army."

The woman laughed. "Then the house with the gray shutters is where you want to go."

"Is Quantrill there?" asked Nettie Gaines.

The tavernkeeper shook his head. "Nobody knows where he hangs out or where the men he rides out with would be."

"But there are folks who do know. I see that by the looks on your faces. Well, I know where to look for them, thanks to you. I'm obliged."

The next morning Lije and Mrs. Gaines started out early. She took a friendly, gossipy leave of the inn-keeper's wife, calling her daughter, thanking her for the food she'd put in the basket, and waving farewell as if she'd known the couple for years and was kin to them.

After they were out of sight of the river and tavern, the woman turned to Lije and said, "I heard somebody riding past the tavern around midnight. There's business going on around here. Did you hear anything?"

"No, ma'am. I guess I slept hard."

She nodded. "Young ones do, old ones don't. Count it a blessing while you can. Are you scared, boy?"

Lije sighed. Yes, he was frightened. What would they find at the house with gray-painted shutters? "Yes, I reckon I am."

"Well, we did just fine last night. Let me do the talking when we get there."

"I plan to, but what'll I do when you're gone?"

"Keep quiet. Listen and watch. And remember, there may be long waits between the time you hear from people who work with Montgomery and Jennison. Be patient. Don't lose heart."

"Wait till I hear the name Nelson or Hawkins, huh?"

"That's right. Don't give up. Maybe you'll hear fast—maybe you won't. When you hear, move fast if you need to. That's why you were given Crow."

"I had a horse I really took to. A Missouri man took him from me. I guess I won't see Banner again."

Mrs. Gaines smiled. "You never know. Horse thieves are not easy to predict in their doings. Where did you lose Banner?"

"Here in Missouri, on a slave raid with my pa."

"Well, Banner could still be here then. Keep your eyes peeled."

"I always do. Banner knows me. I taught him some tricks."

"Don't try to get him to do any if you see a bushwhacker riding him. Otherwise you could have a hard time explaining it if anybody asks you about the animal. Don't make up any stories on the spur of the moment. Don't get caught in lies."

Lije sighed again and said, "I'm looking for a man named Prentiss and one named Hamilton."

"Maybe you'll see them. Maybe not. Missouri has a lot more pepole living in it than Kansas does."

"I know, but there don't seem to be many in these parts."

That was true. Lije drove for a couple of hours, and all they saw were more trees and one abandoned farmhouse. Another one they passed looked as though it had been burned out some time back. Jayhawkers came here, thought Lije with grim satisfaction.

Three hours of travel went by in silence until Mrs. Gaines remarked, "The road we're on has been traveled a lot. Look at all the hoof marks in the dust and how the bushes are trampled down at the sides."

"Bushwhackers?"

"I'd say so, and not too long past—maybe a couple of days ago or less. And there were quite a number of them. They weren't riding single file."

The house with gray-painted shutters was more than a cabin, as Lije had imagined it would be. Sheltered among oaks at the sides and rear, it boasted two chimneys, a story and a half, and a veranda with benches and a spinning wheel on it. Lije figured it must have five or more rooms—it was that large. Deep woods and gently rolling hills stretched out on each side of its cornfields. The corn growing was bright golden-green. Black people were working there, stooping and weeding.

"Slaves!" Lije mumbled to his companion.

"I see them. Expect them here. Don't let on how you feel about them."

Lije took the wagon up the road to the veranda, where a fair-haired woman sat at the spinning wheel. She put down her work and got up. Shading her eyes with her hand, she called out, "Will, somebody's coming."

Two men came through the front door. The first, a big man, had long dark hair, a beard and mustache, and wore a red shirt. The other was taller, thinner, and more interesting to look at. His nose was long and his hair sandy, but his mustache was straw-colored. That mustache was so long, it was tied around the back of his head. Two big pistols protruded from the scarlet sash tied around his waist over a frilled white shirt. A Bowie knife stuck out from each boot top.

The first man, who had just one pistol stuffed into his belt, looked Lije up and down and then called out, "Who'd you two be and what brings you here?"

"Business," cried Mrs. Gaines. "I come looking for Mr. Quantrill. Is that you?"

"I ain't Quantrill." Both men stepped down off the veranda.

Boldly, Nettie Gaines now asked, "Well, if you ain't, who would you be?"

"Allen's my name, Will Allen." The dark-haired man came up to the wagon, walked around it, and laughed.

"What do you want with Quantrill? He don't deal much with granny women."

Nettie Gaines snorted. "I fetched my grandson to him to be made a man of. I fetched him out of Kansas where he and me don't belong no more. We hold with slavery and Missouri thinking."

"Tell us some more," said the taller man with a grin.

"I surely will, mister."

Sitting next to Mrs. Gaines, Lije heard her tell the two men and the blond woman exactly what she had told the tavernkeeper the night before. She finished with, "So I fetched Red to Missouri. He's fit to grind coffee beans if you don't like that chore, ma'am."

After all three Missourians had laughed, the woman said, "Red, take off your hat and show them your lovely locks."

Lije did, and the man with the huge mustache chuckled. He said to him, "You got a good-looking head of hair and a good-appearing horse there, but can you ride and shoot straight?"

"Yes, sir," Lije managed to say. "My grandpa taught me good."

"What's your name, mister?" asked Mrs. Gaines.

"Jim, Jim Hickok's what I call myself." He turned to the other man. "I say we take him off his poor old granny's hands."

Nettie Gaines said, "If you do, you'll have my blessings and my prayers forevermore."

Will Allen shrugged. "I reckon we could use another rider."

"Will my boy get to Quantrill?" asked the old woman.

Allen replied, "Maybe, maybe not. But we could get some use of him. Have you got any money to leave with him, granny?"

"I'll give you a five-dollar gold piece. That's all I got. You Missouri men wouldn't rob a poor old woman, would you?"

"Never, madam, never!" Hickok bowed, his hand over his heart.

Mrs. Gaines reached into her pocket, gave Hickok the tiny gold piece, and ordered Lije, "Kiss me good-bye, but don't you dare bite me the way you did when you was little. Give me them reins. Get your horse and blanket roll and stay here with these folks. Behave yourself. Try to make me proud of you."

As Lije kissed her on the cheek, she leaned over and whispered. "Remember 'Nelson' and 'Hawkins.' God keep you!"

"Are you leaving so soon?" asked the blond woman.

"Why wait around? I got to get back to the river before dark." She smiled. "There could be bushwhackers around."

"There could be at that," agreed the man who called himself Jim Hickok. Then he said a strange thing. "How about a kiss for me, too, granny?" he asked and sprang to the wagon seat, embraced the old woman for an instant, his head next to hers, and smacked her on the cheek before leaping down.

Lije saw the astonishment on Nettie's face as she said, "Do tell! You're a mighty bold one, ain't you, kissing granny women. *Jim?* I won't forget you."

She clucked to the mare, wheeled the wagon about, and started down the road at a trot, leaving Lije staring after her. From what he'd seen of her, he was sure she'd get back safe and sound to Lawrence. She could talk her way out of any trouble that might come along.

But what about him? Could he? Lije felt a finger of icy fear touch his heart. Now that he was really here, things looked a lot different than they had in Lawrence. He felt himself trembling inside and prayed it didn't show. Could he do what the Jayhawkers asked of him? He'd seen men like Allen and Hickok among the Jayhawkers. They looked pleasant, laughing and peacefully leaning against hitching rails, but they were dangerous. They had a certain glint in their eyes. These two Missourians had that sharpness, and a person who knew what to look for couldn't miss it.

Chapter Nine

THE STRANGER
IN THE ROAD

*A*llen told Lije where to take his horse, then went into the house with the woman. Chewing on a straw, Hickok walked leisurely beside the frightened boy. At the shed that served for a stable, he told him, "The big chestnut horse over there is mine. The white one belongs to Allen. There's a place for yours, Red. The others we got are in the pasture."

Looking around, Lije asked, "Ain't there more of you than just you two and the lady?"

Hickok laughed. "Sometimes there's more. Sometimes there's less. There's woods around where we can put plenty of horses."

Lije bit his tongue. He shouldn't have asked this right off. It could have sounded nosy. Besides, he was supposed to be a no-talker. He turned to look at the back of the house. There were a woodshed, chopping block and woodpile, rain barrel, corncrib, well, wash tubs, and smokehouse not far off. This was a good farm, older and better than those he had seen in Kansas.

He asked, "Where'll I sleep, mister?"

"Wherever the lady says. I think she'll expect you to keep the woodbox filled for her. The way your grandma talked about you, I wonder if you can be trusted with an ax. She says you're a wild one. How good can you shoot, Red?"

"Folks say good enough."

"We'll see. I'll go out and test you tomorrow morning. I see you got yourself a pistol. That's good. We don't use rifles much, mostly Navy Colt pistols."

Lije asked, "How come you don't use rifles?"

"They get in the way, they're so long. We like to work up close. I shoot with both hands. How about you, left or right?"

"Just my right one."

At the very moment Lije was removing Crow's saddle, there came the sound of a pistol being fired from behind. Lije whirled to see Will Allen, pistol in hand.

He was hanging halfway out over a windowsill. Below him lay a white hen, her head blown off. Allen yelled, "I got her, Jim. She finally come out from under the barn. Tell the boy to pluck her for the pot."

Lije turned wonderingly to Hickok. "In Kansas they wring chickens' necks or chop off their heads."

The man smiled. "That wasn't no ordinary bird. That hen crowed like a rooster. In Missouri they say it's bad luck to have one of them around, so Will got rid of her. Tend to your animal and then tend to the hen. Use the tub over there for the feathers. Save the giblets. I'm partial to the gravy."

Five minutes later Lije sat alone plucking the hen. Some of his fear was fading. So far he'd been accepted. The bushwhackers had put him to work. Hickok had gone into the house by the rear door. As Lije jerked off white feathers, he wondered at his first minutes with these bushwhackers. He hadn't expected to chop firewood or do kitchen chores, but if that's what they wanted him to do, he'd do it. He had to be accepted by them.

After a stewed-chicken supper, Lije slept on the floor of a little room. Hickok also slept in there, though he had a bunk. It was bare, not even furnished with a basin or towels. They washed out back in basins set on a bench. While Hickok snored, Lije lay awake thinking. By now he'd gathered that the men were the blond woman's guests. Was she a bushwhacker, too? All he knew was her name, Lotta; and she didn't talk much.

Breakfast was biscuits, gravy, eggs, and ham. After eating, Lije and the two men saddled up and headed north, following Allen's lead to a river that fed into the Missouri. They rode along its banks until they came to a place where a lightning-struck oak lifted its bare limbs to the spring sky. On the west side, its bark had been riven into one long, black cleft by the bolt that had struck it.

The bushwhackers stopped here and dismounted. After tying their horses to nearby trees, they readied their pistols. Lije did the same. His fingers could not help shaking, but nobody seemed to notice.

The targets were limbs of trees, floating logs in the river, birds on branches or in the sky—whatever struck the men's fancy. First Allen, then Hickok stood and shot, one after the other. Jim's marksmanship astonished Lije. He never failed to hit his mark, popping bark, whirling logs, bringing down a crow on the wing.

"Now, Red, you shoot," ordered Allen.

Biting his lip, Lije lifted the heavy pistol, drew a bead on a half-submerged log, and fired. His bullet hit off-center, but hit it. Next he fired at the branches of a dead oak and hit two out of three. Because of the noise, no birds were left to be seen, and Lije was grateful he needn't shoot any.

111

"He shoots good enough," said Allen. "Let's get back to Lotta's."

They mounted again with Lije trailing. They'd gone a mile or two when Allen reined his white horse about and came back to Lije. He said, grinning, "Now let's see how good you can handle a horse, boy."

With no warning, he hit Crow a cruel blow with his whip. Startled by the pain, the horse reared, pawed the sky with his hooves, and jolted down, with Lije hanging on for his life. Then Crow began to run toward the west, galloping out of control.

Behind him, he heard Allen bellow, "If he don't never come back, we won't go out hunting for him, Jim."

Crow ran, ears back, tail straight out, and mane beating into his rider's face. Lije sawed on the reins. He prayed the black wouldn't work the bit over his teeth and become unstoppable, or take Lije under a low branch or knock him off in a thicket.

The horse raced for miles with Lije hanging on, sliding dangerously to one side, then the other. Crow came at last to the edge of a fast-moving stream and came to a halt so suddenly that Lije almost pitched over his head. The animal stood, sides heaving, flanks covered with white lather.

Lije dismounted cautiously, patted the horse, and looked in rage at the bloody place on the horse's rump where Allen had quirted him. Suddenly Crow lifted his drooping head to scent the wind. He nickered. He was looking over the stream at something he'd smelled.

Lije looked too. There on the opposite bank under hickory trees stood another horse, a red bay. Lije's heart stopped. Banner! Yes, by the Lord, it was Banner. He pursed his lips to whistle to him, but did not. They weren't home in Kansas now. He had to keep his head. Besides, Banner had a rider. Lije peered harder. The rider appeared to be a boy, slenderer and younger than he was. He wore a big brown felt hat that covered his whole face.

"Hey, who'd you be?" shouted Lije.

There was no answer, not even a wave of a hand. Instead, the rider turned Banner away from the stream, gave Lije and Crow a long look over his shoulder, and went into the trees and out of sight.

Stunned by all that had happened so fast, Lije stood motionless for a time beside Crow. Then he began to walk the horse along the river. When Crow had cooled off, he'd water him and mount up again. They'd go upstream to where this stream probably fed into the river by the lightning-blasted oak, then ride south to the house with the gray shutters. Lije glanced at the sky. They weren't lost. They could make it back by midday, and that would show Will Allen that Red could ride as well as shoot.

*   *   *

Nobody paid much heed to Lije when he returned. Allen and Hickok were sitting on the back porch smoking pipes while Lotta hung out laundry.

"Have a nice ride, Red?" asked Hickok with a grin.

"I saw some of the country I ought to get to know, I reckon."

"That's good, boy."

Curious about Banner and his rider, Lije said innocently, "I spotted a red bay while I was gone, a fine-looking horse. Who owns it, do you know?"

"Is it worth stealing?" asked Allen. "I fancy bay horses." He called to the woman. "Lotta, do you know of any red bays around here?"

"No. I know all the folks, but I don't know all the horses. Maybe it's a new one somebody got. There's buttermilk and corn bread on the table for you, Red. Go eat if you want to."

"Thank you, ma'am."

Wishing he could hit Allen the way he'd struck Crow, Lije averted his eyes as he went inside the house past the man. He couldn't let him see the hatred in them.

Hickok got up and followed Lije inside. While the boy poured a cup of buttermilk from the pitcher, Jim leaned against the wall next to the big iron stove. Silent for a time, he asked, "Who was riding this horse you saw?"

Lije shrugged. "I dunno. It appeared to be a boy, younger and littler than me."

"Where'd you see him?"

"Across the river from where my horse stopped galloping. We didn't say 'howdy.' He left and then I did, too."

Hickok nodded. "Will Allen says you'll do. Him and me are going away together later on today. He wants you to stay here with Lotta, a widow woman. She was his sister-in-law."

Lije said, "I'll do what I'm told to do."

"That's fine. That's how folks keep out of trouble."

Though he welcomed their absence, Lije found life dull with the two men gone. Lotta's slaves lived in cabins behind the house. They were field hands who never came inside. When Lije walked near them, they moved away, never looking him in the face. How he wished he could tell them he'd known and spoken with John Brown, but he dared not. He had to leave them strictly alone. He sat on the veranda or back porch whittling, doing small chores the woman set him, and keeping as quiet as possible.

Four days after Allen and Hickok had ridden away, Lotta told Lije after breakfast, "I'm tired of the sight of you underfoot. Go saddle up your horse and take him for a ride. I reckon you won't get lost, since you found your way back here before. Go in another direction this time, Red. You ought to learn the Big Sni country good as you can."

Lotta sighed. "Why couldn't your old granny have fetched me somebody who opens his mouth more than to say 'yes'm' and 'no, ma'am.' You ain't no fit company at all, are you?"

"No, ma'am. That's what I been told back in Kansas. I guess the cat got hold of my tongue early."

She waved her apron at him. "Oh, go on. I've got some spinning to do today."

Lije was pleased. He wanted to see more of this stream-crossed, rolling country, and Crow could use some exercise. The horse's wound was healing fine. It didn't curb his stride at all as Lije put him into a mile-covering canter riding south by east. He'd thought of going back to where he'd seen Banner, but gave up on the idea. That had been days ago, and Banner's rider hadn't been eager to make his acquaintance then. After the long canter, Lije put Crow to a steady trot and came out onto the road he'd been glimpsing off and on for a while. He reckoned it was part of the same dirt road he and Nettie Gaines had traveled on, but could not be sure. Whatever it was, it was used a lot, judging by the hoof marks in its soft dirt. He and Crow moved along it, with Lije looking for houses or chimney smoke, but he saw nothing until they came to a bend and suddenly found their way blocked.

A battered old black-and-red wagon pulled by a big dappled gray horse was stationed in the bend sideways. As Lije approached, he saw that the wagon bore the words, "Mordecai Silver, Merchant," in faded gold letters. Lije smiled. He knew about such wagons. Kansas had them, too. Peddlers traveled in them from farm to farm, selling calicoes, needles, thread, spices, pins, candy, and whiskey.

Lije took Crow to the side of the wagon, where a gray-bearded man in a shabby black-and-white-striped frock coat and black stovepipe hat sat sunning himself. He turned to stare at Lije.

Before Lije could greet him, the dark-eyed man ordered, "Take your hat off, my lad."

Lije gaped. There weren't any womenfolk here that he could see. Why should he do that?

When Lije didn't do as the man said, he ordered, "Get your hat off. I want to see your head."

Though Lije was getting angry at the man's tone, he did what was asked. He took off his hat and let the bright sunshine pick up the deep red of his hair.

The peddler grunted and asked, "You'd be the one they call Red?"

"Yes, sir, I am."

"Then you're the one I've been waiting for. They figured you'd be on one of these roads sooner or later. I've covered them all, and now I can leave. First, though, I've got something to say to you."

Lije took Crow closer, then said, "I ain't got no money to buy anything, mister."

"I don't aim to try to sell you anything. I want to say just one word to you—Nelson."

"Hawkins," replied Lije, breaking out in a perspiration of excitement. This man had come from the Jayhawkers.

"How do you fare with Quantrill's Missourians, Red?" The peddler didn't seem one bit excited.

"All right. They're keeping me on."

"Good. Now from here you ride around the countryside to a river north of here, where you'll find a dead oak killed by lightning."

Lije nodded. "I know it. I was there a couple days ago."

"Better and better, my lad. This is what you're to do. When you find out when and where the bushwhackers plan to raid or attack a town in Kansas, go to that tree and leave a message in the cleft. Don't ever use names. Write "Somebody" when you mean Quantrill. We aren't so interested in the names of the other men. Have you got a pencil and paper?"

"No."

"Here." Mordecai Silver gave Lije a tablet and a small pencil. "Keep these in a saddlebag. All you have to write is where they plan to go and when, and then you skedaddle back to them. Somebody will be watching the tree and will pick up your note after you're gone."

Lije asked, "Was somebody watching when I was out practice shooting with them two bushwhackers?"

"Not then, but there will be someone there from now on. You won't see whoever it is, and you don't need to know them, either. They'll change from time to time. You be careful, my boy. Keep your mouth shut and your ears open. Do what you're told. I hear you're with Will Allen."

"Yes, sir."

"What men have you met?"

"Only Allen and Jim Hickok."

"Well, you'll soon be meeting a man called Frank James and a little dark man I saw but don't know. They're hard cases and bushwhackers, all of them. You haven't met Quantrill yet?"

"No, sir, but they talk about him. How do the bushwhackers work?"

"They ride to a rendezvous when they're summoned. When they ain't out riding, they hide out together in five or six different places and come out thirty strong. When they're done, they split up and go back to their hideouts in twos and threes and fours. You're part of Quantrill's band right now, even if you haven't set eyes on him. Stay with Allen and Hickok."

As the peddler took up the gray's reins, Lije asked, "Will I see you again, Mr. Silver?"

"Maybe, but if I come to sell some lace someday to Miz Lotta, remember that you do not know me!"

119

"No, sir, I won't know you."

"All right. I'll be on my way, then. Good luck. You're a brave lad and I'll make a good report of you." He held out a dry old hand. Lije shook it. Then the man said, "Don't ever offer your hand to any outlaw bushwhacker. They don't shake hands. Don't make yourself noticed by being different, Red."

With that, the peddler swung his shabby wagon around and started off down the road in the other direction.

Lije sat Crow for a long time, looking after him, feeling lonesome and sad. Well, the Jayhawkers hadn't forgotten him. He'd heard sooner than he'd expected. He had his work cut out for him, and Banner could be somewhere not far away.

Chapter Ten

QUANTRILL

*J*ust as the peddler had predicted, the two men he'd spoken of turned up at Lotta's in May, riding slowly through her fields. Frank James was not much older than Lije was. He appeared to be around twenty and was tall, lanky, fair-haired, and blue-eyed. The smaller, darker man had longish black hair and a broader face. Lotta told Lije, "These are friends of Will's, Tom and Frank. They'll be staying to supper, Red. Kill two chickens for me."

"Sure, Miz Lotta, and I'll pluck them, too."

Frank James said slowly to the woman, "This boy's

got a real head on his shoulders, ain't he? There's nothing I like better'n chicken feathers for supper."

Lotta shrugged. "Jim Hickok's took a fancy to him. Leave him alone. He does his chores all right, and that's all I care about. Don't talk to Red unless you want to waste your time. He ain't got nothing worthwhile to say."

The men didn't. They spent the rest of that day on Lotta's veranda, ate supper, slept in one of her upstairs rooms, and rode off before dawn.

May 1861 passed slowly. Will Allen returned late in the month to report that Arkansas, North Carolina, and Virginia had seceded from the Union and that Tennessee was on the point of doing so, too. He said men were joining the Confederate army all over the state and that there could be fighting in the state real soon. That excited him.

And so there was. On a stifling hot June day, news came that there'd been a fight between Kansas and Missouri men at Booneville, a half day's ride away from Lotta's. The rider who fetched the news was the same dark bushwhacker who'd come with Frank James. He was exhausted, his horse nearly dropping from over-riding. While Lotta poured whiskey for him, Lije tended to the spent horse, then came into the house.

Lotta and the man were in her parlor, talking. In

the kitchen Lije put his ear to the wall between the rooms and listened.

He heard the man tell her, "The plain truth is, ma'am, that our soldiers lost. The Yankee soldiers shoot better'n we thought they ever could. Besides, they had cannons. We made a stand down the slopes of a hill, but men from St. Louis came up and shot us down. They knew what they was up to. It only took twenty minutes. We were driven off and our supplies were captured. The Yankees even ate our breakfasts."

"You were there with our men?" asked Lotta.

"I surely was."

"What about Will and Jim and Frank and Quantrill?"

"I didn't see them there, but I seen Quantrill later. He sent me to tell you to get places ready for ten men or so to stay hid. Can you do that?"

"I got tents that can be put in the woods. There's food enough in the smokehouse and root cellar. How long'll the men be here?"

"Not long, not that many of them. Ten men will be noticed where two or three won't."

"Where are you bound to next?"

"Back to Quantrill. He says there'll be another scrap soon and we'll win this one."

"Another one in Missouri?"

"Yes."

Lije held his breath. Would he say where? No, he

didn't. Instead he said, "This ain't good whiskey, Lotta, just bust-head whiskey."

And she laughed.

Two days after the bushwhacker had left, hot June turned into breathless July. No more riders came. Lotta sat on her veranda fanning herself, while the slaves moved slowly about in her fields, sometimes singing. Lije watched them from the front steps below her, pitying them but not daring to show it. The woman was not cruel to them, just indifferent. Lije wished Jayhawkers or Redlegs would come to rescue them, but guessed that with him here they wouldn't. All he could do was wait for Quantrill or other bushwhackers to show up—wait as the woman waited.

The two of them got a surprise in mid-July. Twelve men in blue coats came riding up her road, halted, and asked Lotta for water to fill their canteens. Yankee cavalry, that's what they were. Lije showed them to the well while Lotta stood on the veranda watching them, not speaking.

Lije asked a young soldier, "What brings you up to these parts?"

"Looking around for bushwhackers. Are there any here?"

Lije shook his head. "Nary a one. Has there been any fighting anywhere?"

As the soldier filled the canteens, he said with a scowl, "Yep, there was on the fifteenth—at Carthage way south of here. That was one we didn't win." He gave Lije a hard look. "We're Iowa Volunteers. I see you got slaves here. We'd take them away from you if Abe Lincoln had told us to do that, but he hasn't. I don't understand you Missouri folks. Your state ain't even seceded from the Union yet, but there was plenty of Missouri men shooting at us. The Rebs had artillery and used it good. We was outnumbered. We lost a lot of men. The horseflies was terrible, too."

Lije's heart sank. Keeping his face unchanged, he asked, "Is there fighting in the East, too?"

"Not yet, but there will be. There's big armies back there getting ready—lots more men than here."

"Soldier!" came a sharp command from a tall sergeant. "You stop that jawing. Fill them canteens and we'll leave. You, boy!" He pointed at Lije. "Get back to your mama."

Lije was about to say Lotta was no kin to him, but thought better of it. He stood watching her as the bluecoats rode past the house to the north, singing a song called "The Happy Land of Canaan."

Near the end of July, Lotta asked Lije to harness her horse to the wagon. She was going to drive to Keytesville, one of the nearer towns. She said she went for coffee, beans, flour, and other supplies, but he guessed from her nervousness that she went for news more than anything else. That's where news came first—to the towns. It could come by steamboat up the Missouri to river towns and be passed along by riders or be carried from the last telegraph station by horsemen.

When Lotta returned, she was wearing a new white straw bonnet with yellow ribbons. There was a smile on her face. As Lije started to unharness the horse, she told him gaily, "There was a big battle in Virginia at a place I never heard of called Manassas. Our soldiers made the Yankees run like scared rabbits. The bluecoats expected to win, and folks came out in fancy carriages to see us Confederates whipped like they was going to a picnic. But they got a sorry surprise."

Lije asked, "Was there anybody we know there?"

She paused, sighed, and said, "Of course not. Virginia's hundreds of miles away. Don't you know that?"

Lije lied. "No, ma'am. I guess I forgot."

"Forgot? You never learned. Unload the supplies after you've tended to my horse. I bought a jug of molasses to pour over our pork and beans. Don't you dare bust it."

On the last day of the month, a stranger came galloping in just at sunset. While Lije stared out a parlor window, pistol in hand, Lotta flew past him to open the door—after she put down the rifle. They were guarding the place more carefully now since the Yankee cavalry had come by. Lotta cried to Lije, "It's my cousin. He's come from Quantrill!"

Quantrill? Lije caught his breath. Now maybe there would be some definite news to write down as a note and put in the oak tree. The news he'd heard before was too vague to pass along.

And that turned out to be the truth. Lotta's fair-haired cousin, Joel, had been sent by Quantrill to tell her that nine men would gather at her house by tomorrow night and would stay only that night. She was to get things ready for them. After passing this information on to her, he left immediately.

While the woman baked and cooked all night, Lije set up two old tents in a grove of black walnut trees not far from the house. He guessed the riders would bring their own bedrolls, but all the same he piled old blankets onto the bottoms of the tents. Would Quantrill be coming with them?

By early morning, men were riding in by twos and threes and singly. All strangers to Lije, all long-legged, hard-eyed men, they had little to say. They ate what Lotta gave them and spent the time playing cards, sleeping, and tending to their pistols and horses.

Lije kept asking himself if he should ride to the oak and leave a note about these men, but decided not to just yet. He wanted to know why they were here and where they were going. Were they going to join Quantrill on a raid into Kansas? He dared not ask.

Lotta's cousin returned with the last man, someone Lije recognized. Jim Hickok. Hickok greeted Lije, tousled his hair, and said, "This here's Red. His granny fetched him to us."

One of the strangers laughed and said, "Lotta told us that and that he ain't got much between his ears but his red hair."

"Mebbe not," agreed Hickok, "but he can shoot and he can ride. I seen him."

"Then he's coming with us," said the cousin.

Hickok sounded surprised. "The boy's supposed to look after Lotta for Will Allen."

The cousin shook his head. "Lotta can take care of herself for a spell. Quantrill said to bring everybody who can cock a pistol and aim it. That means this kid, too."

Hickok asked, "What's Charley up to, a raid or a battle?"

Lije caught his breath. Would he hear now? Would he have a message worth writing?

All the cousin said was, "Jim, you know better than that. Charley don't tell what he's up to. He said to gather up all the men in these parts we could and ride out at dawn heading south. Somebody'll meet us along the way and tell us where to find him."

Hickok grunted. "Now don't that sound just like Charley, though?"

In his mind Lije wrote a message. "Somebody is gathering many men to ride south. I go too." That's what he'd leave in the oak tree—if he could get away.

Late that afternoon he found the opportunity he needed. Lotta sent him to tell a slave out in the woods felling timber for firewood to come back to the house. He rode out on Crow, found the black man, and gave him the message. After galloping Crow as fast as he could, he wrote the note and shoved it out of sight in the crack, then gave Crow a nudge with his knee and raced back. A glance over his shoulder showed him no movement other than the flow of the river and the leathery rustling of tree leaves in the summer heat. Yet the peddler had promised the tree would be watched!

Nobody said anything to him when he got back except Jim, who looked hard at Crow and remarked, "You been riding that animal pretty hard in such hot weather. Don't do it again."

"Yes, Mr. Hickok, but if I'm to ride out tomorrow, he ought to get some exercise."

"All right, boy. There's no debating that."

Six days of riding in fearful heat and staying overnight at farms whose owners were loyal to the South brought Lije and his companions to the neighborhood of Springfield. The day after they left Lotta's, they'd been met by a man who told them their destination and the reason for coming. Armies, Federal and Confederate, were gathering around Springfield. A battle might be in the making.

A battle? Lije hadn't counted on a real battle. Being forced to go on a Kansas raid, maybe—but a battle here in Missouri! Just the thought of it made his mouth as dry as the dust that rose up in waves under Crow's hooves as he rode south behind Jim Hickok.

Quantrill's tent camp lay in very hilly country a distance southeast of the town. Hickok and the others rode into it just before dark and were welcomed by torch-carrying bushwhackers who demanded to know who they were.

"Jim Hickok—not his ghost," thundered the man. "I know you and you know me. You're Willie Allen and you're Cole Younger and you're Frank James. But maybe you don't know all these fine, loyal Missourians," and he rattled off the names of all those with him, ending with "Red Quentin, the kid here." Then he asked, "Is Quantrill around?"

"He is, and he wants to see you," Allen told him. "He's eating now, but he'll come out to tell you what we'll be doing in the battle."

Battle! Lije heard the word again with horror. Hickok asked, "Where are the bluecoats?"

"Somewhere around here. They know we're here, and we know they are, so there's no cause not to have cook fires and hot grub."

"Get down and rest your horses," Hickok ordered his men. "Go get some food." He turned to look at Lije, laughed, and said, "You stick with me once you've hobbled your horse to graze. Your granny sent you to Quantrill and gave me money for him, so he ought to get to see what a present she gave him."

Quantrill at last? Lije did what he was told, then made his way through a large number of bushwhackers to find a portly Confederate captain dressed all in gray, standing beside Hickok and a tall, slender young man. Lije could not hear what the soldier told them, but whatever it was, it didn't take long. His face was sour as he mounted his waiting horse and rode off.

"Red, you come over here," called Hickok.

Lije walked to Jim and looked up into one of the strangest faces he'd ever seen. Charley Quantrill had a long, thin face, an unusually long neck, fair hair, long blond whiskers at the sides of his face, and a red mustache. His mouth was wide and crooked, his eyes a pallid blue. He wore a black slouch hat with a gold cord, a red shirt, gray trousers, and brown cavalry boots. Two pistols had been jammed into his belt.

He looked down at Lije and said in a tenor voice, "Are you the lad your grandma brought to me?"

Lije took off his hat. "Yes, sir, I am."

"Do you want to fight a battle?"

What should he say to this? At last he said, "If it'll help win the war, I reckon so."

Quantrill smiled, or rather one side of his mouth lifted a bit. Then he turned away and went into a tent where a kerosene lamp burned, yellowing the white canvas.

"Come on and eat," Hickok ordered. He strode to a cook fire, pushed Lije down, and left him, going off into the dark beyond the tents.

"Who'd you be?" asked a young man with long, golden locks.

"Red Quentin. I come with Hickok."

As Lije spoke, he was given bread, then a slab of beef dripping with fat. It came on the end of a Bowie knife held by a man acting as a cook.

The young bushwhacker gave his name and added, "I come from Cass County, southwest of here."

Lije mumbled, "I used to be from Kansas. I been living up in the Big Sni country up near Keytesville lately. That's where Will Allen lives."

The young man smiled. He leaned forward. "I seen you talk with Quantrill. He's a real fine talker, he is. He used to be a schoolteacher, so he knows a lot of fancy words. You heard much about him?"

"No, but my folks felt respect for him."

The Cass County youth chuckled. "I don't see how he ever got to be a teacher unless it was somewhere nobody knew him. I hear tell he was some hell raiser as a boy. He used to tie two cats together by their tails and throw them over a clothesline to scratch and bite.

He nailed snakes to trees, and one time he painted a cow red."

As he ate, Lije felt nausea rise in his throat. He couldn't laugh the way the other bushwhackers around the fire did. He asked, "Why'd he paint a cow red?"

"For devilment, I reckon."

"Paint costs money. It ain't for cows."

Another bushwhacker grinned and told Lije, "Quantrill's going to be made an officer in the Confederate army real soon. We're going to be named 'partisans for the South.' That means we'll be soldiers—sort of."

Lije swallowed with difficulty and asked, "Are we going to get gray uniforms?" How it would gall him to put on Confederate gray!

"Probably not. We'll wear red sleeve bands or something like that to show we're partisans."

Lije nodded, relieved.

Another man said, "We won't look like regular Confederates, but I bet we shoot better than they will."

"Probably a whole lot better," boasted the Cass County man. "Have you ever heard the Yankee song, the one about old John Brown?"

Lije said cautiously, "Uh-huh, I heard it sung in Kansas."

"Did you ever see John Brown there?"

Lije coughed at the unexpectedness of this question, choked on a bite, coughed some more, and lied, "Nope."

"I'll bet you heard all about how he come to Missouri to steal our slaves. But when you lived in Kansas, did you ever hear what him and his boys done to five men they come upon here?"

Lije nodded. "I heard he shot and killed them."

The golden-haired bushwhacker shook his head. "You heard wrong, my friend. What the Browns did gets kept quiet over in Kansas, we hear. Them poor Southern men got hacked to pieces, hacked up like sides of beef, hacked with swords."

"*With swords?*" Lije looked at him in horror and then at the half-raw meat he'd tried to make into a sandwich. His pa had never told him that! "Did John Brown do that?"

"He didn't. His sons did. Quantrill says John Brown's the real reason for this war we're in. He was a crazy old galoot slave stealer, good for nothing but hanging from a rope."

Lije's mind went back to his cherished memory of John Brown standing among the slaves he had just freed. The boy sensed the story of the swords could be true, but could Brown have agreed to such a horror? Perhaps he could. Lije remembered the fire in his old eyes as the man had given him his blessing. Biblical warriors used swords, didn't they? Though he felt ill, Lije went on chewing and managed to drink a tin cup of the bitter, dark coffee that was handed to him.

When it was gone, he returned the cup, saying "Thanks," stood up, and mumbled, "I got to see to my horse. He came a distance today."

But Lije didn't go in search of Crow. He hurried past the tents and beyond them to where it was dark. He found a tree, leaned against it, and vomited again and again. Clutching at his empty, aching stomach, he held onto the tree for support and thought about the things he'd just heard—about the man he'd idolized and the men he'd been sent to spy on, about his pa's murder and the burning of the Tulley farm. What could he do? He was among bushwhackers now. He'd just have to put a ramrod alongside his spine and take his mind off John Brown and swords. He'd better focus instead on his ma and sisters and the Cousinses, and how he'd try to keep them safe by his work. He'd have to watch himself all the harder, now that he was in Quantrill's camp. That man's eyes were the dullest, coldest, and cruelest he'd ever seen—harder than Frank James' or Will Allen's or Jim Hickok's. He'd once read in a schoolbook that the eyes were the windows of the soul. His teacher had explained that this meant the soul could be seen and judged in them. If that was so, it didn't appear to him Quantrill had one.

And tomorrow there'd be a battle he might take part in.

"Lord," he prayed, "look out for me. I'm in so deep

here and I don't know anybody else who'll help me."

While he stood trying to pray, Lije saw something through the shadows—the glint of a bridle. Then there came the muffled sounds of hooves. One rider and one horse. As they passed, he recognized Jim Hickok, no doubt on some errand for Quantrill. What devilment was he up to, going out riding in the night?

Chapter Eleven

WILSON'S CREEK AND BEYOND

For the rest of his life, Lije Tulley would remember that September day at Wilson's Creek, Missouri, remember it as he would remember John Brown's blessing and his pa's death. He could not recall any details, but memories of the brutal heat and swarms of flies, his thirst, the shouts of men and screams of wounded horses, and his wordless terror would haunt him always.

The battle started at dawn as a cannon duel between the two sides—great booming roars, belching flames, and puffs of smoke. The bluecoats' attack took the rebels by surprise. Lije watched with the bushwhackers from the top of the bluff as the Federals pushed back the enemy through a cornfield. The fighting continued on the slopes of the hill. Mounted on Crow, Lije reluctantly charged downhill with Quantrill and his men. They were shooting and howling as they descended over the battlefield below, where the gunsmoke was so thick that Lije saw only flashes of fighting. Wherever the smoke cleared, there were soldiers in blue and in gray, cursing, shouting, yelling, stumbling, and falling wounded or dead. Some were knocked aside and downed by the rush of cantering horses. Then the smoke would drift back to cover the horrors. Crow leaped over fallen men, who reached for Lije's stirrups to claw him off and kill him. Bullets whizzed past him like furious darting bees, although he kept his pistol in his belt.

His heart in his mouth, Lije made it unscathed to the timber on the opposite side where Quantrill ordered a halt. There they waited in the growing heat, coughing at the fumes, listening to the din, watching the Confederate infantry march down Oak Hill and fight man-to-man in lines only a hundred and fifty feet apart, appearing, disappearing, and reappearing as the smoke came and went. The courage of both armies made Lije's eyes ache with unshed tears. He sat on his horse, trembling, and felt Crow tremble, too. Crow wanted to run away as much as he did. Lije prayed

Quantrill would not send them back over the battlefield again. If so, he would refuse to go. Let Quantrill shoot him. It would be a better way to die than getting shot by somebody in Union blue. But the bushwhacker did not order his men back into battle.

By eleven-thirty, it was over. The Union forces had lost, mainly because their commander, General Lyon, had been killed, and his men had run out of ammunition and retreated. The South had won, but at a high cost, indeed. Almost a quarter of all the soldiers on both sides who had fought at Wilson's Creek had died.

That dreadfully hot afternoon, Lije rode with Jim Hickok over the battlefield. Snorting, Crow daintily picked his way through the dead and wounded men. While other bushwhackers were joyful, Hickok seemed somber. Lije could understand why. Never had the boy seen so much blood or so many open-eyed, open-mouthed men staring dead-eyed at the yellow sun.

Suddenly Lije made a strangled, muffled sound as Crow stepped over the body of a lanky, dark-bearded man wearing a blood-soaked gray officer's coat. Lije had recognized him. It was Judah Hamilton, the man he'd seen from the loft the night John Brown had come, the man who'd ordered the Tulley homestead burned.

Hickok asked, "You gonna be sick, Red? Go ahead. Throw up. Nobody'll blame you."

"No, sir, I ain't sick. I don't have any breakfast in me."

"See somebody that you know down there on the ground?"

"Yes, sir, that's it. He wasn't no friend to me, though. Just a man I saw one time."

"Yes, I seen a couple I knew, too. Well, you and me, old General Price's huckleberry cavalry, we're alive, ain't we? Did you shoot anybody while you was riding along with Quantrill in his cavalry charge, Red?"

Lije had been expecting the question and had his answer ready. "I don't think I hit anybody, there was so much smoke. I fired one time, though." That part was true. At the very end Lije had fired into the ground, just in case anybody looked into his pistol. He now asked, "What'll Quantrill do now?"

"Follow up the whipped Yankees. But he told me he's sending you and some of the others back up to Lotta's. The war might come up there later on, and he wants to make sure there's lots of food laid by. Them men need to get in crops and tend to the hog killing this fall."

Go back to the North? Lije's heart leaped, but immediately afterward he felt guilty. How could a person feel happiness where so many men lay dead around him?

He told Hickok, "I don't ever want to be in no more battles. That made me sick enough to puke. I don't want to see no more dead men."

"That remark shows me you got more sense than

your granny gave you credit for. Men ought to hate war, but some just love it. They're crazy mad."

Lije asked, "Will you go back to Miz Lotta's, too?"

"Not right now. I drop in and out here and there."

"You mean like last night? I seen you leave our camp."

Hickok looked surprised. He stared at Lije. "Did you? Well, I had errands elsewhere."

"For Quantrill, huh?"

"That's right, Red."

"When'll I start back north with the others?"

"Tomorrow morning. That's what Quantrill says."

As Lije lay in the tent he shared with Frank James and some of the other bushwhackers, who went on incessantly about the day's victory, he brooded over the fight and seeing the dead man who had wronged his family. He didn't take any pleasure in it, not at all.

Though he didn't want to see Quantrill again, he did, just after breakfast. And what he saw turned his stomach into such a knot he couldn't eat the rest of the day.

Passing by Quantrill's tent, Lije spied a thick-bodied graycoat officer entering it. He didn't see his face, but the voice stopped Lije in his tracks. He recognized it. It belonged to Prentiss, the Missouri planter who'd shot down his pa and Jake Cousins.

Lije squatted near some bushwhackers who were

shooting dice on a blanket and pretended to be interested in the game until the man came hurrying out, looking neither to the right nor the left. Yes, it was Prentiss for a fact. Lije trembled.

One of the dicers noticed and said, "Ain't you over being scared of the battle yet, sonny?"

Lije answered, "It ain't that. I never been this far south in Missouri before, and today I seen two men I knew up north." He shaded the truth swiftly. "Both of them were dead on the ground. Ain't it odd I seen two of them?"

How he wished Prentiss had been lying there, too. Hate stabbed him as he watched the officer mount a roan horse and ride away. He asked the dicers, "Why do the army officers come to Quantrill?"

The bushwhacker called Cole Younger laughed. "To try to give him orders. Mebbe he'll follow them. Mebbe he won't. He wants to be a big army officer hisself, but they ain't made him one. We ain't so popular with the regular army, it appears to me."

Lije said nothing to this, but got up and went to where Crow stood grazing. It was time to bridle and saddle him. First, though, he flung his arm around the horse's neck and leaned his head against Crow's warm flesh. Homesick, this touch comforted him. Crow was a Kansas horse.

He whispered to him, "We're going north again,

you and me. We'll be closer to home up there than we are here. You did just fine at Wilson's Creek, even if we rode for the wrong side. No horse could'a done better than you."

For a long moment Lije thought hard, considering the fact that he'd encountered both Judah Hamilton and Prentiss here at Wilson's Creek. It seemed an odd coincidence, but was it? He'd been summoned down here as a bushwhacker. The two men had gone into the Rebel army, so why shouldn't they be here among other Missouri soldiers? Yes, it wasn't so unnatural after all.

Somewhat to Lije's surprise and discomfort, Quantrill came to say good-bye to the northern partisans. He walked up to the mounted men and said, "Thank you for coming when the South called you. You did well yesterday. Be sure that I'll call on you again. Any time one of you wants to cut loose and come join me, he'll be welcome. You'll be seeing me again, I promise you."

The man next to Lije laughed and said, "For a Missouri bushwhacker, you sure talk mighty fine, just like the schoolteacher you was."

Quantrill smiled at him. "Yes, I teach other things these days. One of these days I'll ride north and we'll go hunting Kansas Jayhawkers." Again he smiled.

Looking at his strangely crooked grin, Lije shuddered. Yes, he believed Quantrill's words. This man would come hunting Kansas men. But when? He needed to know.

Lije dared ask, "When'll you come, Mr. Quantrill?"

The man turned his odd eyes on him. "When the weather's better for that than for fighting battles. Cannons and heavy wagons don't travel fast in deep mud."

"Winter," Lije told himself, rejoicing at the answer to his question.

The man who had appointed himself leader of Lije's group raised his hand and called out, "Let's get on our way."

As they rode single file among the tents, Lije spotted Jim Hickok. The man was looking into a mirror set onto a fence post, shaving. He didn't see Lije, but Frank James did. He was sitting against a tree next to Will Allen, who was whittling a whistle from a twig.

Frank James lifted his hat mockingly to Lije as Allen called out, "If you can remember, tell Lotta that I fancy blackberry jam."

Lije nodded. "Yes, sir, I will."

Attracted by the conversation, Hickok turned around, gestured at Lije with the long-blade razor, and then went back to his shaving.

It took longer returning to the house with the gray shutters. There was no hurry this time. The bushwhackers detoured to little towns, where they boasted about their great deeds at Wilson's Creek and how many Yankees they'd killed and wounded. Some bought red neckerchiefs and new spurs with the money Quantrill had paid each of them. Lije bought only a scarlet satin ribbon to braid into Crow's tail. He sat outside the saloon, admiring the effect while the others drank up the rest of their pay. Once when a rider had gotten too drunk to sit his mount, Lije helped tie the bushwhacker onto the horse and then led the mount behind Crow.

Lije knew that Missouri hadn't seceded from the Union yet, and he looked for signs of patriotic feeling for the North, but he saw none. Perhaps the people of the hamlets and farms they rode past knew bushwhackers when they saw them and were wary of them, wary enough to keep their dangerous sentiments to themselves.

Lotta's farm was unchanged. She was spinning on the veranda, getting thread ready for homespun clothing, when he sighted her down the road. She saw him at the same time and left her wheel to come down and greet him.

Her first question was, "Where's Will Allen? Is he all right?"

"He stayed down near Springfield with Quantrill and Hickok and the others. I reckon he'll go where they go."

"Did he give you a message for me?"

"Yes'm, he surely did," said Lije, and he repeated the man's words.

She laughed, then asked, "Did Will send you back here?"

"No, Quantrill did. He said, 'Tell Lotta to keep everything ready. We'll be coming north.' Quantrill said he'd come hunting Jayhawkers near winter."

"Did he?" The woman's face brightened. "Good. There's been slave stealing around here, some miles to the west. They didn't come here, though."

Lije wanted to grin. No, Mr. Montgomery wouldn't send raiders to this place.

He told her, "We were all in a battle."

"Yes, I heard about it. Was Will hurt?"

"No, ma'am, nobody you know was."

"Thank the Lord. And we won, too!" She turned away to her wheel, adding, "Stable your horse and be sure the woodbox is filled. Wash yourself good on the porch so you don't smell up my kitchen. You smell of horse sweat."

"Yes'm, I reckon I do."

The next morning Lotta ordered Lije to exercise her roan mare.

Glad of the chore, Lije took paper and pencil from Crow's saddlebag and stuffed them inside his shirt before he bridled and saddled the mare. He rode first to the lightning-blasted oak, fished out the paper, and wrote, "Somebody plans to come here to fight Jay-hawkers in late fall or winter." He folded the note and put it into the cleft.

Next he took the roan off a distance and dismounted. After tying her to a tree in a thickly wooded grove, Lije climbed the tree. Had somebody been watching? Would somebody come riding for his note?

Suddenly Lije froze on his perch, peering through branches already losing their leaves to autumn. In the distance he saw a gleam of red moving against the green-and-dull-gold landscape. Straining his eyes, he saw a red bay, his Banner, trot up to the oak and watched as the rider reached inside the tree and took out the note. Yes, it was the same rider, the one with the large hat, that he'd seen weeks before. Lije saw him unfold the note and read it, then look off to the west.

Who was this boy? He had to be on the side of the Kansans or he wouldn't come to the tree. But how had he got hold of Banner? The Prentisses had kept his horse when they'd killed Pa and Mr. Cousins, and the Prentisses were Confederates. He'd seen old man Prentiss in a gray uniform. Had the Prentisses sold Banner or traded him? Had this boy stolen him? If he had, good for him! It had rankled Lije to think that his horse belonged to the man who had killed his father.

Where was the boy taking the message? Would he be going over into Kansas or just passing it to somebody else? Lije went on watching.

After the rider finished reading his note, he put it into his vest pocket, then took off his hat and fanned his face with it. Long, black hair fell down the rider's back to below the shoulders.

Lije gasped. This wasn't a boy at all. It was a girl. A girl? A girl coming to get his note? A girl sent by the Jayhawkers? It couldn't be. She had to be some girl out riding who had seen him hide the note and rode up out of curiosity to read it. And she had his horse!

Anger consumed Lije. He skinned down out of the tree, freed Lotta's horse, and jumped on as the horse ran out of the sheltering trees. Leaning along the roan's neck, Lije raced toward the girl.

Hearing the thud of hooves, she slammed her hat onto her head again, dug her heels into Banner's flanks, and with a yell started him into a gallop to the west.

Lije grinned. It was the first real grin he'd had on his face in a long time. He whistled long and shrill, and Banner did just what the boy had trained him to do. He came to a sliding stop. Nothing would budge him except the second whistled command. The girl could yell at him, spur him, or whip him, but he'd stay put.

She did none of these things. She stayed on Banner, turning her head to glare at Lije as he rode up to her. Dark eyes, shining bright with fury, looked at him. He gaped. She had one of the prettiest faces he'd ever seen.

It was heart-shaped, with pink cheeks and a rose-red mouth.

Suddenly Lije saw that her small hand held a derringer and that the tiny but deadly pistol was trained on his chest.

She said, "You leave me be!"

Lije put his hands up. He told her, "That's my horse you're on. His name's Banner. I taught him to stop at my whistle."

"Unteach him," ordered the girl coldly.

Lije told her, "I seen you take something from the oak tree."

She flared, "You put it there. I saw you. You gave it up."

"Why'd you take it out, then?"

She took a deep breath and, still glaring, said, "Because Mr. Nelson Hawkins told me to get it and take it somewhere else."

Nelson? Hawkins? John Brown's names! Lije let out his breath. "Put the derringer away," he said. "I'll teach you the whistles for my horse. What's your name?"

"Mary, Mary Dent. Who're you?"

"Elijah Tulley, but I'm called Red Quentin here in Missouri."

She nodded. "They told me you had red hair. We was all told that. I ain't the only one who keeps watch for you. It's a good thing your red hair is long enough to show under your hat. If it didn't, I might have shot you." Saying this, she put the derringer into her trouser pocket.

Then he asked, "I'm sure glad you didn't shoot me. We're on the same side. How come you got my horse?"

"Somebody I know stole him from some slave hounds and gave him to me."

"Well, those slave hounds took him from *me*. I'll let you ride him for now, seeing as how you know the right names and you're a girl."

"Oh, thank you, kind sir," she said mockingly. "I really must be on my way. Now if you'll kindly teach me those whistles."

Lije nodded. He whistled a second time, but a different note, and Banner came over to him and rubbed his head against Lije's knee.

The girl smiled. "I reckon he is your horse. He's a good mount. I call him King."

Lije liked that name. He reined Lotta's horse away and asked, "Can you whistle those two notes?"

Mary Dent laughed. "Can I? Sure I can. I suppose you think girls can't whistle."

She whistled, making Banner prick up his ears. She asked Lije, "Will Quantrill come before the end of the year?"

"I heard him say he will. I was at Wilson's Creek with him."

Mary's eyes widened. "You were there at the battle?"

"I was, but I only fired my pistol one time, and that

150

was in the ground. I had to ride with the bush-whackers."

Mary Dent said nothing but held out her hand in sympathy. Lije rode closer, took it, and held it. It was a small, rough hand, tanned by the sun.

She didn't snatch her hand away. She waited until he let go, gave him a long look and a little smile, and said, "Nelson." Reining Banner about, she whistled the second note and started off, moving fast.

"Hawkins," whispered Lije as he watched Banner disappear over the brow of a small hill. Mary, Mary Dent. Who was she? Did he dare ask Lotta at supper?

Lije rode the roan slowly, his mind conjuring up memories of the pretty girl. Her nose was small and straight, and her eyes were the darkest black he'd ever seen. He reckoned she had some Indian blood. Lordy, to think that she would really have shot him with that derringer of hers. She sure was a brave girl. But she would have to be to be doing such a dangerous and important job for the North. She was pretty and smart, and her calloused hand told him she must work hard. He'd never met a girl like her before. He had to find out more about Miss Mary Dent!

Chapter Twelve

THE NEWCOMER

*I*t took Lije a week to get up the nerve to ask Lotta about Mary. One evening between bites of hominy, he said, "Miz Lotta, do you know a family around here by the name of Dent?"

"Dent?" She stopped eating and thought for a minute. "There's a woman named Dent, half Osage Indian, they say, and a boy living some miles from here. I never met them. I hear tell they're standoffish. They keep to themselves in the hollow in the woods where they live. I see them now and then in Keytesville selling baskets of eggs. The boy's younger than you."

152

Boy? Lije smiled.

The woman asked, "Did you run into a Dent?"

Lije told her a half truth. "I met up with a boy when I ran your horse for you last week. That was all."

The woman sniffed. "Well, don't bring him here. He looks like a horse thief to me."

"No, ma'am, I won't fetch him here," Lije said, and at the same time promised himself that he would see Mary Dent again.

In late September, Cole Younger and one of his brothers stopped at Lotta's briefly. As Lije watered their horses, Younger filled Lotta in on the bushwhackers' activities. He told her, "Quantrill went to Lexington with General Sterling Price. You know where that is, just a half day's ride from here. The town full of Union men held out a little more than a week against us, but then we took it. Quantrill figures there'll be more fighting around Springfield later on, so he don't plan to come up here for a spell yet."

Lije reflected. This wasn't news for the tree.

Lotta asked Younger, "How's Will Allen?"

"Your brother-in-law is fine and dandy."

In turn, Lije asked, "How's Mr. Hickok?"

Younger didn't take offense at being addressed by Lije. He laughed. "Him? He comes and he goes, he goes and he comes. I figure Quantrill knows why. We don't. There's some news to tell you that ain't war news. The end of next month the telegraph is going to be stretched clear across the whole country. It'll go from Denver to Sacramento. That's way out in California."

Lotta said, "Thanks for the news. We don't hear much. Is there fighting in the East?"

"Nope. Cold weather'll be coming on. That'll stop the armies, but it won't stop bushwhackers and Jayhawkers. Horses can move fast so long as there ain't deep snow."

Lije nodded. That was true enough, and Quantrill would know that.

The bushwhackers came unexpectedly on a rainy night in late November. Twenty riders arrived with Quantrill, their horses splashing in the mud in front of Lotta's house. Will Allen, Frank James, and his yellow-slicker-clad gang were with him, but no Jim Hickok. Quantrill didn't stay long himself. He drank a toast to Missouri's having finally seceded from the Union, thanked Lotta for her hospitality, and rode off. Everyone but Will Allen and Frank James rode with him. By now Lije knew that it was typical bushwhacker behavior to split up to be less noticeable.

Just before he left, Lotta asked him, "Are you going Jayhawker hunting, Mr. Quantrill?"

"More than likely, ma'am, when the spirit moves

me," was all he told her. Then he tipped his hat to her, mounted, and led his men out at a trot.

A week later Quantrill sent a rider asking the men at Lotta's to meet him at a ford at the Big Sni. Lije was not asked for, so he stayed behind. He had raced to the oak tree with the message, "Somebody gathering riders along the Big Sni," but had not dared linger because Lotta had not sent him on any time-consuming errand. He didn't see Mary Dent or anyone else.

It was a couple of days before Will and Frank returned to Lotta's place. They'd been to Kansas and had fought with Jayhawkers and burned some houses. As Allen rocked in a chair in Lotta's cozy, warm parlor, he said, "Quantrill shot down two Jayhawkers hisself. We heard that one of them Kansans a while back hit a Missouri woman in the face with a pistol. We hit him with one. That ain't anything men like us put up with. Shooting menfolk is one thing, but we'd never shoot anybody who wears a sunbonnet any more than we'd use swords like John Brown did when pistols or a rope will do."

Lije had heard enough of this. He got up and told Lotta, "I'll go put blankets on the horses. It's going to be powerful cold tonight."

"That's right," agreed Frank James, "but that won't stop Charley Quantrill from calling us out. Froze-up ground makes for fast riding."

*   *   *

And so it happened that cold, wet winter. Several times Quantrill sent riders for Allen and James, and they'd return to tell where they'd raided and burned. The bushwhackers struck like lightning, moving swiftly to rob the mails and steal good horses. Lije knew because of their speed that any messages he was able to send would be picked up after the bushwhackers had come and gone.

Three times he saw a tall man on a sorrel horse take his message and ride west. Only once, the fourth time, did he see Banner and Mary Dent. She was so bundled up against the freezing wind he knew her only by her small size and the fact that she rode his horse.

Christmas that year was lonely and sad for Lije. He hoped some message about his family would come to him by way of the oak, but none did. He spent the day in the stable currying Crow and the other horses, while the bushwhackers celebrated on Lotta's whiskey and wild turkey dinner. Lije had had little appetite for the food. He kept thinking about his family and friends in Lawrence. What were his ma and sisters and the Cousins family having for dinner? Lije was sure his folks were thinking of him. What kind of story had the Jayhawkers told them about why he was away so very long buying horses for the U.S. Army. Wouldn't they be shocked if they knew he'd been at Wilson's

Creek? And what were Mary Dent and her ma doing this Christmas day?

Spring came late, with a great deal of rain that made the rivers swell and the earth a quagmire. As for Will Allen and Frank James, Lije grew very weary of their company. Their drinking, poker playing, and constant cussing disgusted him more and more. Lotta disliked these things, too, and asked them to stop. Nothing much came of her request, though they did watch their language a bit to please her, being respectful of women.

Late in February Quantrill came by again to collect James and Allen.

When Lotta asked him where they were headed, he told her, "We're going to join a Southern army. We aim to fight wherever we're needed. The war will heat up again. Farewell to you, ma'am. Keep the faith."

Now Lotta took to driving her wagon to town for whatever news she could glean. In April she came home to tell Lije of the battle of Shiloh that ended in a "draw" between the armies, and in May she brought the news that there were battles in Virginia and that the city of New Orleans had been taken by Lincoln's forces.

One day later that month, as Lije hacked away in a wood near the house, cutting down small trees to make a new corncrib, he heard the whistle he used to stop Banner. He dropped the ax and turned around to see a bareheaded Mary Dent astride his horse in a glade some twenty feet away. He saw her look carefully around, then whistle and nudge Banner forward to where he stood.

She told Lije, "There's a letter come to you from Kansas. I been hanging on to it for a while because I don't see you at the tree no more."

Lije said, "There ain't any news about bushwhackers to put there, that's why, Mary."

"Here's your letter. You're to read it, then tear it up so it won't be on you. I can stay only a little while. It's too close to the house." Suddenly the girl laughed and leaned from the saddle. "Don't you want to pet your horse, Red?"

"Sure I do." He patted Banner's sleek hide, grinning, then said, "You take good care of him, Mary. I want him back someday."

"Maybe," teased the girl. Then, laughing, she swung Banner around and rode off, leaving him alone, letter in hand.

Smiling, Lije tore open the letter. It was a short one, dated Christmas Day, 1861. It read:

> Dear Son,
> We're all fine here. The bonnet shop does
> well and supports us. Your sisters are in
> school. Ira Cousins works for Mr. Bass now,
> at the stable. We'd like you to write us.

158

Aren't you weary of buying horses? When
will you come home? Mr. Montgomery says
it could be a long time. I hope not. Dr. Jennison told me he'd see to it this letter gets to
you. Be sure and buy long underwear and
wear it October to May. Don't take up smoking. It will stunt your growth. We all hope
you had a good Christmas.

Your loving ma

Lije read the note three times, then tore it into tiny
pieces and stuffed them under an old fallen log where
they would never be found. Because of his ma's note
and Mary Dent's visit, Lije felt just fine. Grabbing the
ax, he swung it with all his might, making the chips
scatter far and wide.

In early September Lije found out about Quantrill's
activities. Via one of Lotta's trips to Keytesville, the
town where Quantrill had been early that summer, Lije
learned that he'd been robbing steamboats on the rivers
and, in July, was in Cass County. Quantrill had also
gone to Independence, Missouri, which was held by
Union men, taken it, and looted it. Furthermore he
had been made a captain in the Rebel army. After that,
he'd ridden to the town of Lone Jack directly below
Independence and fought Union army guards there,
too. He'd been plenty busy, thought Lije angrily. Lotta

159

also brought news of heavy fighting in the East, once more at Manassas, and this time the Rebs had won another victory.

Then, one night in late October, Will Allen came riding alone to Lotta's to stay for a while. He'd taken a bullet in one leg when Quantrill raided a Kansas town called Olathe. He told Lotta that Quantrill was leaving Missouri for a time. He planned to go to Richmond, Virginia, the capital of the Confederacy, and ask for a commission as a general.

Allen told the listening woman, "I don't know that he'll get up that high in the Army. The regular army men don't take to us bushwhackers much. There's an officer name of Prentiss I met who surely hates dealing with us since Wilson's Creek. He don't try to hide it neither."

Surprised to hear the name, Lije flinched and looked around, but saw no one had seen it. How he longed to ask about Prentiss' whereabouts, but how could he?

Lotta wanted to know, "Who'll be in charge when Quantrill's gone?"

"Maybe Frank James or Hickok, or maybe Bill Anderson, the one they call Bloody Bill. He's joined up with us. He hates Yankees and he ain't afraid of nothing. He takes enemy scalps and hangs them off his horse. If he comes here, mind what you say and do. There ain't no telling about him."

"You don't take to him, Will?"

"I don't hold with craziness, not John Brown's kind or Anderson's kind. There's things I could tell you, but they ain't for women to hear."

Lije couldn't go to the tree that night, but the next morning he rode Crow and left a message saying that Quantrill had gone to Virginia. He watched for Mary, but she didn't come. No one did, and he wondered why. Then suddenly from the top of a distant hill he saw a glint of light—the flash of a mirror, or was it a ray of sun on a spyglass? Yes, somebody was watching. Rising in his stirrups, Lije waved.

As he rode back, Lije tried to remember his school-room map of the country. How long would it take to get to Virginia? It should take weeks of traveling. That could mean some peace and quiet for the Union army with Quantrill gone, but this winter would probably fetch more bushwhackers to Lotta's farm. Maybe Frank James and Jim Hickok would come again. It wasn't so hard for him to be around Lotta, but with the men there, he could again become the butt of their jokes. He'd already been picked up and tossed into the horse watering trough, and he could have his head shoved into the rain barrel when he didn't get out of the way fast enough. One of them had already threatened to do that.

One night a few weeks after Allen came, Lije was sitting on the veranda steps, admiring the effect of the full moon on Lotta's slave-harvested hemp and cotton fields. Shadows from her fences painted black stripes on the pale ground. Lotta came out, wrapped in a shawl over her long nightdress. She seemed cold and didn't notice Lije at first. She started when he said, "Miz Lotta?"

"Is that you, Red?" And she sighed.

He asked, "Is Will Allen going away again soon?"

"No, not with that bullet wound he's got. It pains him a lot if he walks too much."

Then she went on as if Lije weren't there. "I hate this war. Will says it'll soon be over. I don't think so. I hate waiting here for him and the others. It'd be different riding with them, but I can't do that. They don't want a woman any more than they want a boy like you, who ain't got much good sense. You and me, we sit and wait. I don't like blood and battles and killing. All Kansas and Missouri have had for nearly ten years is hate and killing. It ain't no way for a person to live, full of hate and fright and worrying about what's coming along next."

"No, ma'am."

"Oh, what's the use of talking to you. All you ever say is 'Yes, ma'am' and 'No, ma'am.' I might just as well talk to the porch rail."

"I'm sorry, ma'am."

Her hand touched his shoulder. "I'm sorry, too, Red. What you are ain't your fault."

When she'd gone, Lije sighed, too. She was right about war, though she was wrong about him being dim-witted. John Brown and Pa's death and the Jay-hawkers had changed him. It had been hard to see the bushwhackers as human beings, but they were. There was sure a lot of bloodiness in people's hearts every-where. It ate a body up. He could see how it gnawed at souls, turning folks into hunting animals.

In early December, Lije sent a Christmas letter with some good wishes, as well as lies about horse buying in Indian lands, to his ma. He also wrote in a P.S. that the man who'd burned their farm had been killed in a battle and that he'd heard it from a wandering hunter. He put his letter in the message oak, and when he stuck his hand in was surprised to pull out a piece of paper that had "Red" printed on the outside.

All it said was, "Merry Christmas to you. The Johnny Rebs lost a fight in Arkansas. Somebody wasn't there. There's fighting going on in Virginia and Tennessee. Cold weather don't stop it." It was signed "M" and below it ran a long line of X's.

Lije chuckled. He got out his paper and pencil and wrote on his knee, "Merry Xmas to you, M., and a lot more X's. Nobody's seen hide or hair of somebody. There's only one man of his where I stay."

Lije was grinning as he rode for Lotta's. By now Crow knew the way to the tree and back. He'd head directly for it each time Lije took him out on the pretense of exercising him.

The new year came in with the announcement Lije had expected for some time: On January 1, 1863, Abraham Lincoln signed the Emancipation Proclamation freeing all slaves anywhere in the United States. In having slaves on her place, Lotta was breaking the law of the land. Lije listened to her and Allen laugh about the proclamation. What did it mean to her, Lotta said, since the South was going to win the war?

Lije longed to tell her slaves what Lincoln had done, but dared not. They eyed him with distrust and moved out of his way, looking at the ground whenever he came near them.

That January was bitter, so cold the creeks froze and tree limbs snapped like pistol shots. Will, Lotta, and Lije stayed in the house, piling wood into the sheet-iron kitchen stove and fireplaces, but still they shivered.

In mid-month, Jim Hickok and Frank James came to the farm on an icy but sunny afternoon. With them was a swarthy young man with masses of coal-black hair and a slender, gentle-faced, blue-eyed youth near Lije's age.

Lotta and Will went out to welcome them, while Lije stood behind them on the veranda, looking on. Hickok dismounted, kissed Lotta on the cheek, and, pointing to the dark man, said, "This is Bill Anderson. He joined up with Charley Quantrill a time back."

"I've heard of you," said the woman as Anderson nodded to her and Allen and then got off his horse.

Frank James spoke up now. He pointed to the boy behind him. "This is my brother. He's had some bad trouble from the Union men, so he's come from Clay County to join us. He shoots and rides good as I do. He was in Arkansas at the battle of Prairie Grove. His name's Jesse. Jesse, this is Miz Lotta and this is Will Allen."

"Howdy do." Jesse's voice was soft and flat.

Frank now pointed to Lije. "That kid there is called Red 'cause of the color of his hair. He was at Wilson's Creek. You two got something to talk about together."

"Maybe," said Jesse.

Lije felt his eyes examining him. He had a sullen air to him that Lije didn't like. Now Jesse looked away to watch his brother dismount.

"Where's Quantrill?" Lotta asked Hickok.

"Still in the East, but he'll be back this spring after he visits his lady love."

"Has he got one?" she asked.

Hickok rolled his eyes. "Charley's got one in just about any town you name. They even spy for him if he asks them to. He gets news of Jayhawkers that way."

Shocked to hear the word "spy" used, Lije sucked in his breath. Recovering his composure, he was alarmed to see that Jesse James had heard him. He was staring in his direction and frowning.

"I've got to be more careful around him," Lije told himself. "He looks like a bad one."

Chapter Thirteen

SPIES AND MORE SPIES

*L*ije learned from Hickok what had made Jesse James turn to bushwhacking. Jesse had stayed behind on the James farm, where they'd once owned seven slaves. He'd been plowing the fields when Union sympathizers came riding in. They started to hang his stepfather, but Jesse's mother kept cutting him down. Then they had beaten Jesse savagely when he tried to rescue the old man.

Lije said nothing as he thought of the whipping he'd got at the Prentiss place. Jesse's stepfather had not been shot dead like Ab Tulley. Jesse had been luckier than he had been.

In the days that followed, the Kansas boy found he didn't take to the younger James brother. Jesse was sly and watchful. Where Frank James skylarked, teasing Lotta and playing jokes on Will and Lije, Jesse took no part in these doings. He never smiled or laughed like youths his own age that Lije had known at school. It appeared to Lije that everywhere he went, Jesse turned up, too. And he was quiet, quiet like the cat his sisters had once owned that sat hour after hour watching in the woods for little birds to fall out of their nests.

It was a big relief to Lije when Bill Anderson complained of crowding at Lotta's and rode to another farm. For a time it appeared that Frank and his brother might go elsewhere, too, but they stayed on.

The next news they received of Quantrill was a letter to Will Allen that the man wrote in March. It said he'd been granted a colonelcy in the Confederate army and that he'd be back in May.

At last some news to take to the oak tree! The Jayhawkers would be very interested to learn that Quantrill would be in Missouri again in the spring.

Hoping to see Mary Dent, Lije saddled Crow and rode through a rainy afternoon to the tree. Jim Hickok and Jesse James had ridden out earlier to Keytesville to buy supplies, plus new high-heeled boots for Hickok and a felt hat for Jesse.

Cold rain dripped down the back of Lije's neck as he sat hunched over, writing a message and thinking of Mary Dent. He wrote, "Somebody's coming here again in two months." He signed it "Red" and under his name bravely added a row of X's. In Kansas that meant kisses. He bet it meant the same thing in Missouri. Reining about, he headed Crow for Lotta's, arriving with his long oilskin coat running with water.

A little later Hickok and Jesse returned, too, with bulging saddlebags. They'd bought not only boots and a hat, but also white shirts, ammunition, horehound candy and peppermints, dried fruit for pies, whiskey, and a black shawl with pink roses for Lotta.

Jesse and Hickok displayed all of this during dinner. Then Jim draped the shawl over Lotta's shoulders, saying, "This is for all your good cooking, Lotta."

Will Allen laughed and all at once asked Jesse, "Have you got a girl back home, Jesse?"

"No, sir, but I got a pretty cousin." Jesse pointed to Lije. "Red's got a girl, though. He puts notes in hollow trees for her. Me and Jim saw him this afternoon. It was raining so hard he didn't spot us riding up, but we seen him." Smiling, Jesse took Lije's folded note out of his breast pocket. He unfolded it and read it aloud.

169

Lije sat thunderstruck with terror. What could he say? He'd been caught red-handed. No one had come to get his message. Of course not! Whoever was watching would have seen Jesse and Jim right after Lije had ridden off and would have wisely stayed hidden.

Will Allen reached for the note, read it aloud again, and looked at Lije. "What're you up to riding out putting notes in trees?"

As all eyes turned to him, all Lije could do was grow pale with fright and confusion.

Suddenly Hickok began to laugh. He boomed, "I seen that note, too. Look at all them X marks at the bottom. Our Red's in love. He's gonna meet some gal somewhere come May and spend a day with her. Ain't that true, Red?"

Lije met the man's eyes. Though his mouth laughed, his eyes did not. They were sharp, warning eyes.

"Yes, sir. There is a girl. I leave her notes."

"A girl? What girl?" asked Lotta. "There ain't many girls around here."

Lije shook his head. "There sure is. I met her out riding one day last year while I was exercising your roan mare."

"What's her name?" asked Will Allen sharply.

"Alice," said Lije, using his mother's name. It was the first one that came to his mind.

"Alice who?" demanded Lotta.

"Alice Nelson. She's sort of new to this part of Missouri. Her pa brought her ma and her here and then went off to the Confederate army."

Jim Hickok snapped his fingers. "That's right, Lotta. Last time I was here, I met up with a woman who said she was new-come. She had a girl with her in their wagon. The girl was a good-looker, honey-haired and blue-eyed." Leaning back in his chair at the kitchen table, Hickok went on. "The name's right on the end of my tongue. Red's right. It is Nelson. I thought it was Hawkins, Mrs. Hawkins."

Lije stifled a gasp and stared at Hickok. Jim continued to look at the ceiling and teeter on his chair.

"You'll bust my chair, Jim," scolded Lotta.

Hickok brought the chair down gently and went on talking to Lije. "Red, you must be new at courting the girls. I wouldn't wait from March to May for kisses from a girl I'd set my heart on. What's wrong with her? Has she got weak lungs that a little rain would bother her?"

Now all eyes were on Lije again. He stammered, turning red. "Yes, sir, she says she's subject to the ague." He'd taken his cue from Hickok. Had he done the right thing?

Frank James warned, "Don't get mixed up with no sickly girl if you know what's good for you."

"Frank's right," agreed Jim. "Quit leaving love notes in trees is what I say, or you could find yourself married up with somebody who'd never enjoy a well day in her

171

life, like the Mrs. Hawkins I used to know. That's how I got the name wrong. This Mrs. Nelson had a sickly look to her that reminded me of the other lady." As he said "Hawkins," Jim's right eye closed in a slight wink.

Lije's spirits gave a leap. Jim Hickok wasn't a real bushwhacker at all. He had to be a spy, too, or he wouldn't have known the secret of these two names. Wait a minute! He'd seen Hickok ride out just before the battle at Wilson's Creek, hadn't he? As a Jayhawker, he wouldn't have taken part in it. He'd have found a good excuse to leave.

Jim got up, stretched to his great height, and said, "I'm going to see to my horse. He's got a cut on one leg. Come along with me, Red, and help me tend to it while I talk to you about girls."

As Lije gratefully rose to follow him, Jesse said peevishly, "I don't think Red's got hisself a girl. How come he calls hisself 'somebody,' not Red, then signs his name Red? And how come she can come out in rainy weather if she's sickly?"

Lije thought faster than he'd ever thought before. "Alice don't like the name of Joshua, which is my real name, and she don't like Red much either. She calls me a special name I don't like, so I won't use it. I use 'Somebody' instead."

"What is it?" teased Lotta.

172

"Sweet Love," said Lije, thinking of the most humiliating name he could imagine.

"Dearie me," crowed Jesse. "Oh, dearie me. Sweet Love! They said you ain't got much sense, and you ain't. No wonder she rides out in the rain. She ain't got good sense neither."

"Come on, Red," ordered Hickok.

Splashing through the rain after the man, Lije arrived at the barn breathless with fright to find Hickok looking sternly at him.

Jim told him, "I saved your bacon back there. I knew all along who you were. Silver, the peddler, told me you were coming. I told that granny woman who fetched you here who I was when I kissed her. I said, 'Nelson Hawkins.' She hadn't figured there'd be another Jayhawker here so soon. She got a surprise. Because you came to stay, I was free to ride around with Quantrill and pass the word of what he was up to all over the state. Keep away from that tree from now on. I bet Jesse will hang on you like glue now to catch sight of your girlfriend. He mustn't see the Dent girl or anybody else who comes to the oak. I'll get word to somebody on our side that Quantrill's due back in May."

Lije asked, "Why didn't you stop Jesse from taking that note?"

"He saw you before I did. He's got eyes good as an

eagle's. I was behind him favoring my limping horse. He'd got the note and read it before I rode up to him. He read it out loud to me. I told him it was a private love letter and to put it back, but he wanted to have some fun with you. He's worse than a copperhead snake."

Lije said bitterly, "He sure did have fun with me. Thanks for helping me out. You think fast."

"So do you. Because they think you can't think, they'll believe what you told them. Thank the Lord you wrote 'somebody,' and not Quantrill, or you wouldn't be out here talking with me. You'd be dead in that kitchen. I'll be leaving again soon. I got business elsewhere."

"Can I go with you, Mr. Hickok?"

"No, you stay here. Go out and chop wood and keep watch. Mary will find a new hiding place to use for notes. She's a smart one and mighty pretty to boot. I knew her pa. He was a U.S. Army scout. He got killed four years ago out west. But watch out for Jesse James. He ain't like his brother. He's got different instincts. Now, let's see to my horse."

As they went to Hickok's horse, Lije asked, "Will Dr. Jennison or Mr. Montgomery send a message for me to come back to Kansas pretty soon?"

"Homesick, Red?"

"You bet I am."

"I can see why. I'll tell somebody you've had a

bellyful here. Maybe they'll call you home, maybe not. You got an in here with Will Allen, and he hears from Quantrill more than most do. You're a brave boy. The way I see it, you're needed right here, Mr. Elijah Tulley."

Lije swallowed hard. It had been such a long time since he'd heard his real name, hearing it came as a painful shock to him.

He mumbled, "I'll stay long as I can stand it. Is your name really Jim Hickok?"

"Yes, it is. I saw no cause to change it. I can see why you did, though, with your pa, Ab Tulley, being shot by Missouri men."

"By Major Prentiss," Lije added bitterly.

Hickok ignored that. He asked, "Are you sweet on the Dent girl?"

"I reckon I am."

Hickok chuckled as he bent and lifted the chestnut's right hoof and set it on his knee. Hickok muttered, "A floating snag nicked him when Jesse and me forded a creek. Remember what I told you, Elijah. You'd do best to lie low here till Quantrill shows up."

"What'll happen then?"

"The Lord only knows, or maybe the devil knows better. Charley will be up to some real devilment, now that he's a colonel in the Johnny Reb army. He'll be hoping that rank will make the army men think more highly of him. They don't take to him, you know."

"I heard that. Mr. Hickok, do you know the Reb officer named Prentiss I just told you about?"

Hickok grunted. "I do. You may hate Prentiss, but he hates Quantrill like poison. You have to give him that. Bushwhacking is the worst kind of war work there is. For that matter, Jayhawking is, too, though there's a better cause behind it. Army men go by rules. They've got their own courts and judges. Some of the night riders ain't much more than animals. They like killing. For all his fancy talk, Quantrill's like that. So's Anderson, and I wonder about Jesse. Now fetch me the horse liniment, Red."

Chapter Fourteen

GENERAL ORDER
NUMBER TEN

*H*alf of April had gone by before Lije had dealings
with the Jayhawkers again. Jesse James was lazy,
and Lije knew it. He'd figured if he went out to cut
saplings for firewood, Jesse wouldn't want to go with
him. Lotta's woodpile was getting lower and lower,
and she was happy to send Lije out with the ax.

The sound of chopping carried for miles, so Mary
Dent could hear it and come to him—and so she did.
She rode Banner to the spot where he stood hewing
down saplings. Throwing the ax down, he ran to her.

Mary stayed on the horse, looking down at him and

smiling. "I seen you at the tree in March, but somebody on a gray horse came up and got the message. Jim Hickok came by later and told Ma and me that you wouldn't be going to that tree no more."

"That's right. Where's Jim?"

Mary shrugged. "I don't know. Quantrill ain't come here yet, huh?"

"No," Lije replied.

"Red, I come to tell you that the Union men are getting tired of women helping out the bushwhackers, hiding them and passing messages for them. They're gonna start putting them women in jails all over the state."

"Lotta, too?" asked Lije.

"Not her, at least not for now. That's because you're there. If you go away, they'll come after her fast. I'm to tell you to stay there till Quantrill comes. When he does, come out here and chop firewood. I'll listen for you, and so will other folks. Someone with the right names will come riding and hear what you got to say, then pass it on."

Lije sighed. So he was to stay. He could complain to her of Jesse James, but what could she do about him? He said wearily, "Mary, you and me ain't old enough to be soldiers. This is no way for people young as we are to be living."

She nodded. "In a way we are soldiers, doing our duty. Ma says so. I hear there are drummer boys and bugle players only ten years old in both armies back East. We're older than that."

Lije came nearer and patted Banner with one hand; with the other he took one of hers. "Are we gonna see each other when the war's over?"

"I think so."

"Have you got a beau, Mary?"

She leaned down, patted his cheek, and told him softly, "I do now. He's the bravest boy there ever was, and he's got hair the color of a rosewood table."

Lije leaned up and kissed her gently on the mouth. She smelled of woodsmoke and ferns and spring flowers. She laughed, then reined Banner around and left at a trot.

Charley Quantrill arrived in May, splendid in an officer's gold-braided gray uniform. He was now a colonel in the Confederate Partisan Rangers. Lotta, Will Allen, and the James brothers admired him as they all sat on the veranda in the warm sunshine.

"How's the war going in the East?" asked Frank James.

"Not so good. We win some and we lose some. I advised President Davis to take the war up to the North this summer instead of fighting around Virginia and Maryland so much. I think that General Lee will do just that. One bold stroke up there could win it for the South."

Will Allen wanted to know, "Have you seen Hickok?"

Lije held his breath. Had Jim been found out?

"Oh, he shows up now and then. He's riding with our army now as a scout. He's seen a lot of the West."

Lije held back a smile. What army was he really scouting for?

Lotta teased Quantrill. "I hear you got a special lady friend, Charley."

"I do, indeed. I spend time with her when my duties permit."

Jesse piped up, "Red's got a girl, too. Nobody here's ever set eyes on her, though. She don't come visiting. She's got weak lungs, and they've both got weak heads."

Quantrill ignored Jesse. He was too young to impress the man, and Lije was pleased. Quantrill said, "The Missouri ladies I know are very loyal and helpful, like you, Lotta. They fetch us food when we have to live in caves like animals. They take risks like you, my dear lady. I pray no harm ever comes to our ladies. If it should, the villain will have me to reckon with. I promise you such men will be punished so they will always remember it."

Lije repeated these words, fixing them in his memory. Tomorrow he would go out to split wood into rails and replace the fence that had been kicked down by one of the horses in the pasture.

This time Mary Dent didn't come to the ringing noises of his ax in the woods. Instead, a tall, thin man wearing ragged clothing and mounted on a rangy black mule rode up to Lije. Once he was at Lije's side, he grunted and said, "Nelson." When Lije replied, "Hawkins," the man said, "Spout your piece, son."

Lije repeated Quantrill's threat as best he could recall it.

The stranger nodded, spat tobacco juice onto the ground, and told Lije, "It's not really news that Quantrill will try to get even with anybody who goes after his women. What is news is that he's back in these parts. Where's he headed?"

"To visit a woman he knows."

The man snuffled. "We know who she is and where she is."

"How's Mary Dent?" asked Lije.

"Who's that, son?"

Lije caught at the mule's bridle. "How's Jim Hickok? And the old peddler Silver?"

"How would they be but fine and dandy, boy?" The man on the mule grinned broadly, showing big white teeth. The grin was as good as Hickok's wink had been. They were all fine.

Fiery hot July brought important news of the war to Lotta's farm. Jesse bought a Kansas City newspaper in Keytesville, and the woman read it aloud.

The paper reported that the South's General Lee had marched up to Pennsylvania to a place called Gettysburg. He fought for a couple of days and lost a great number of soldiers, then went back down to Virginia. A Union general named Grant had taken the port of Vicksburg on the Mississippi River. Confederate forces had failed to take Helena and Fort Gibson in Arkansas.

When Lotta had finished, Will Allen whistled and said, "It don't look so good for us right now."

"The war ain't over," scoffed Jesse.

Frank James volunteered swiftly, "Charley Quantrill's going to do something to even things up with the bluecoats. All we got to do is sit tight and wait for him. He'd have heard this news, too, and I bet you a ten-dollar gold piece he's pondering how to do it right at this very minute. And whatever he decides to do is going to make the North shiver in its boots."

After a long silence, Lije asked Lotta, "You need some more wood cut, Miz Lotta? The corral gate and hayloft need fixing up."

She sighed. "That's our Red for you. The war's going bad, Quantrill will call you out again, and all he thinks of is the corral gate and the hayloft. Go on. Take the ax and go. You'll sweat half to death, but that won't bother you. Lord, there ain't one breath of air coming through here to blow those accursed flies away. They're like to eat a body to death."

Thirty minutes later, Lije, pouring sweat, was felling a tree when the same man on the same big mule came to him down a narrow, winding path through the trees.

He said, "It's hot to come out. You got a message for me?"

"Frank James said because of the way the war is going in the East, Quantrill's going to do something soon that'll hit the North powerful hard."

"That figures. So he's riled up? He's gonna be more riled when the women who have been helping him are rounded up by the law. That'll happen right soon. Wives, mamas, and sisters will be going to jail. There'll be a special order about that. It won't set well with their menfolk. Ain't that what you heard Quantrill say?"

"It sure is. How's Miss Mary Dent?"

The man chuckled, then said, "I don't see no harm in telling you now. She and her ma went back to Kansas. The Jayhawkers thought it was time for them to leave. It's almost time for you to light out, too. Once you find out what Quantrill's up to, tell me. Then head for Kansas yourself. You've been here a long time. It ain't wise to leave any one soul in one place too long."

Leave? Lije's heart soared. Saddle Crow and ride out of here forever? What joy!

He said, "Do you reckon Quantrill has another battle in mind here in Missouri?"

"Maybe he does. So long. You be careful."

Saying this, the stranger reined his mule about and let it pick its way neatly up the trail.

Lije went back to chopping the tree. Mary was safe. The war was going well for the Union, and with any luck he could soon be out and away, his work for the Jayhawkers done here.

Once he'd seen his family and the Cousinses, he would find out from Dr. Jennison or Mr. Montgomery where Mary and her ma were. Lije began to whistle the gayest tune he knew, "Weevily Wheat."

Lije Tulley's contentment grew when he later learned the details of General Order Number Ten, which struck at the bushwhackers through their womenfolk who lived in Union-held territory. It stated that any woman who sympathized with and aided the partisans was to leave Missouri at once with her household goods, food, and animals. Those who didn't go would be shipped south.

Before that order even came out, Union soldiers had arrested and jailed women allied with prominent bush-whackers. Frank and Jesse's female relatives had been jailed, and so had three sisters of Bloody Bill Anderson and two cousins of Cole Younger.

And then something dreadful and totally unforeseen happened that stung the bushwhackers to a fury. It turned out that Anderson's sisters and Younger's kins-women were held on the second floor of an old brick building that had been judged unsafe. On the thirteenth of August, the building collapsed and the third floor fell into the second. Four women were killed, including Cole Younger's cousins and one sister of Anderson's. Another sister of Anderson's was crippled for life.

This is what Quantrill had been waiting for! He and Anderson went mad with rage.

Riders were sent to homesteads all over western Missouri with orders from Colonel Quantrill for his followers to gather at a prearranged rendezvous. A man came galloping through the summer heat on a lathered horse to Lotta's veranda, shouting out, "Hey, Will Allen, Frank, come on. The colonel wants you right now. He's gathering men at Pardee's place."

Lije came to the open parlor window to listen while everyone else hurried to the front of the veranda.

"What's up?" cried Allen.

"Quantrill wants you to mount up and join him near the Kansas line. You know where. You won't need food, just your pistols." The rider grinned. "He plans to get even for what the bluecoats done to his ladies. Yankees killed them when a jail fell down."

Though his heart had begun to pound, Lije thought fast. Here was his chance! While the enraged bushwhackers oiled their pistols and got ready to go off with the rider, he would slip out the back way, saddle and bridle Crow, and ride him to the woods to summon the stranger on the mule. Once he'd told his news, he'd make a break for freedom, riding fast as he could for Union-held Kansas City. From there he'd cross the Missouri River and be home in Kansas.

He moved stealthily through the house, opened the back door, and ran to the corral.

Suddenly he heard a soft voice asking, "Where do you think you're going?" Jesse James came out through the back door smiling, pistols in both hands.

Lije stammered, "I was going to get all the horses ready."

"In a pig's eye, you was. You're a coward! What you were really going to do was sneak away by yourself so you don't have to fight again. Wilson's Creek must have been enough for your lily-white liver. I'm on to you, Mr. Sweet Love. Mr. Quantrill wants *everybody*. That's you, too. There's only one place you're going to ride to, and that's Lawrence, Kansas."

"*Lawrence?*" exclaimed Lije.

"You bet, that's where we're going. Charley Quantrill's had it in mind to clean out John Brown's town for a long time. Other men figured it would be Kansas City, where the jail collapsed, but it's not. Charley hates Lawrence and them abolitionists. They got banks and emporiums and money aplenty there. He seen it all. Now you saddle all our horses, including yours. I'll stand right here and make sure you do it right and proper."

And Jesse did. He ordered a slave to come help Lije tighten the cinch on a horse. At this moment Lije whispered what he'd wanted to shout for months. He told the slave, "President Lincoln set you and all the slaves in the South free last New Year's Day. Run away north. I'm telling you the truth. We're all leaving here now, so this is your chance to go. Get away from here."

Lije's reward was first a look of astonishment, then a grin.

"Thank ya," whispered the man. "I'll tell the others. Mr. Allen, he trying to talk Miz Lotta into selling my boy. We'll go tonight 'cause there ain't to be no moonlight."

"Good. Good luck to you."

Chapter Fifteen

HOME

*T*wenty minutes later Lije found himself riding out with the bushwhackers. They rode in pairs, Jesse at his right hand and ever watchful. God in heaven, there'd been no chance of his getting a message to anybody. Could Lawrence be prepared for Quantrill? He prayed that they were. Maybe some other Jayhawker spy had given them warning.

Lije's heart ached as he later sat by a campfire watching bushwhackers ride in from all over Missouri. The wild man, Bill Anderson, came with the scalps of Union men in his saddle bags. He displayed them proudly to everyone. Forty men rode with him, and another partisan chief came with a hundred. Quantrill himself had a large number.

They all rode to Lone Jack next, camped at noon, and at night rode on toward the Blue River. To Lije's horror, there they met up quite by accident with a hundred graycoat Confederate soldiers under the command of a colonel and another officer Lije instantly recognized as Major Prentiss. Lije heard Quantrill loudly invite them, "Join our raid on Lawrence," and heard the colonel accept. At daybreak, fifty more bushwhackers from Bates and Cass County rode up to join the others at a spot only four miles from the Kansas border.

Four hundred fifty men bent on attacking Lawrence camped all day at this spot. Lije was sent to fetch water for the horses from a nearby stream. As he went about the camp, he was sickened to see that some of the bushwhackers were wearing blue Union jackets, taken from prisoners or men they had killed. Nausea rose in his throat at the sight.

Carrying water, he deliberately passed by the two Confederate officers who spoke quietly a distance apart from the bushwhackers.

Prentiss, he saw, had a dark look on his face. Lije heard him say, "A curse on this Quantrill! I don't mind attacking a fort of soldiers, but I don't like coming down on a town of civilians. Dr. Jennison burned Dayton and Columbia in Missouri last year, and I hated that. Now Quantrill wants to burn Lawrence. I hate these partisan rangers!"

"Who doesn't hate this kind of war, Major?" said the colonel. "But my men are just recruited. They need a taste of action."

"This won't be action. These men are wolves. It'll be murder."

"You know, Major, there are Yankee soldiers in Lawrence. Maybe they'll fight. . . ." The officer's eyes fell on Lije, who ducked his head and went past him swiftly.

The boy set the buckets down and leaned against a tree, confused. This Missourian, who'd ordered his pa and Cousins shot for trying to steal his slaves, surely hated bushwhackers, too. At one time it would have been easy to shoot this man down, but not now, however wrong and sinful it was to hold people in slavery. Prentiss thought of his slaves as "property" and defended them as the Tulleys would have defended a cow someone was set on stealing. To him, the Jayhawkers were just thieves! Shaking his head, Lije picked up the buckets at a bushwhacker's call and walked on to water the man's horse.

Flying their black flag, Quantrill's band rode ten miles into Kansas. They stopped again and at nightfall rode out again. Some Union soldiers challenged them but were put off when the partisans, wearing Union blue, claimed to be U.S. Cavalry riding to the blacksmith in Lawrence. Kansas farmers were dragged out of bed at pistol point to lead the bushwhackers in the black night.

Lije thought constantly of escape, but rode surrounded on all sides by Quantrill's men, some of them riding asleep at times, tied to their saddles. Always there were enough of them awake to see Lije and shoot him if he tried to leave. And Jesse watched!

Quantrill's men came in sight of Lawrence at five in the morning. They reined in a distance from the sleeping town to check their pistols and ammunition and see to their saddle girths. As he sat Crow in the fresh August breeze, Lije felt his heart swell with love for his ma and sisters and for the Cousins family. Love was so mixed with terror that he could hardly breathe. It was clear to him that Lawrence wasn't expecting the bushwhackers. If it had, there would be pickets around, horsemen watching, waiting to race back with warnings. It was up to him to do that—give the warning! To him, Ab Tulley's son, John Brown's "Joshua"—if he died for it!

Suddenly Lije put spurs to Crow, and the horse sprang forward at a great, surprised bound. Riding Crow he'd be first into Lawrence. He'd wake everybody up!

Trusting to Crow's speed, he sent the horse into a

gallop. As he entered Lawrence, he fired his pistol three times into the air and yelled at the top of his lungs, *"Quantrill! Quantrill!"*

Nobody shot at him from behind. The bushwhackers thought he wanted the honor of being the first man into the city. They streamed in at a gallop behind him, yelling, "Quantrill! Quantrill!" too.

The first thing they struck was a tent camp of sleeping Union soldiers. "Kill them! Kill them all!" rang out Quantrill's hoarse bellowing. Not bothering to call the soldiers out, the bushwhackers spurred their horses onto the tents, crushing the tents and the men inside.

Then the surge of partisans came thundering up Massachusetts Street, shouting, cursing, firing their revolvers, while their leader went on screaming, "Kill them! Kill them!"

Lije, a little ahead of the galloping horde, but with a young bushwhacker, a stranger to him, on a fast mount at Crow's heels, saw his chance and took it. He reined the wild-eyed black to the right edge of the host of riders, falling back a bit, colliding with the young bushwhacker, knocking his horse aside, and dashed along the side street to his mother's milliner's shop. He'd watched for the sign he'd known she would put up. There it was in fancy blue letters: "Bonnets, Laces, Feathers and Trims—Cousins and Tulley, Proprietors."

He leaped off Crow, slapping him on the rump to

make him run, jumped up onto the porch, flung open the back door, and darted inside. An instant later the young bushwhacker galloped past the half-open door but did not see Lije there. His horse sped along, chasing Crow.

Alice Tulley was piling kindling into the stove. Her mouth fell open in fright, then amazement. *"Elijah?"*

"Ma, Ma!" he called to her. "Quantrill's come here. Hide me, hide me fast!"

Mrs. Cousins, attracted by the voices, came hurrying in with a wrapper over her nightgown and her hair in a braid. "My God, it's Lijah. What's all that racket outside?"

"It's Quantrill, the bushwhacker," Lije told her. "There isn't time to explain now. I got to hide. They don't kill womenfolk, but they'll shoot me down. Hide Ira and Lucas, too. Hurry! Hurry!"

"The cellar!" cried Mrs. Tulley.

She ran through the back door onto the porch and jerked open a trapdoor. Lije dived down its six steps, then heard it slam shut over him and heard something pushed over it.

From where he lay in the cold darkness, surrounded by last year's vegetable crop that kept over winter, he could still hear what was going on around him: the crackling sounds of pistol fire, the high-pitched screams of women and children, the hoarse yelling of men, and the drumming of hooves that shook the earth and filled the air. Soon he began to detect the odor of burning wood as the bushwhackers began to fire the town, as he knew they would.

After a half hour of terrified waiting, there came a pounding on the floor above and the sounds of deep voices that made Lije move farther back into a corner. He guessed what made the pounding—musket butts. *Rebel soldiers!* Bushwhackers didn't carry muskets, just pistols. Oh, dear God in heaven, they were going to search down here! Would the Southern soldiers kill women and girls? They said they never did, but would they here? Where were Ira and Lucas hidden? One thing was sure—bushwhackers would kill him in a minute as a deserter. Lije began to pray as he drew his pistol from his belt.

He heard a woman's cry and knew it came from his mother as the trapdoor was flung open. She cried, "There's nobody down there, soldier!"

"We'll be the judges of that, ma'am. Our orders are to round up any menfolk we find. Corporal, you keep her and these other womenfolk out of the way. Give me that lantern. I'll go."

Lije trembled as he watched the high black cavalry boots come down the steps. The soldier stopped at the bottom and held out a lantern at arm's length. Its beams fell directly on Lije sitting in the corner, holding his pistol on the man. At the same time, it illumined the man's face. Oh, Lord in heaven! It was Prentiss!

Lije froze, speechless. No, he wouldn't beg this man for mercy! But he couldn't pull his own trigger, either. The officer he'd hated for so long held the pistol on him for what seemed like forever. Suddenly it fell to his side and slapped against his leather boot.

Lije heard him mumble to himself, "He's only a boy. I don't care if my order is to shoot all the men in this town. I'm not going to kill him. God, I hate this business. Don't you fire on me, son, and I won't fire on you."

"All right," stuttered Lije.

Prentiss now called up loudly, "There's nobody down here," and climbed back up the steps. This man had taken Ab Tulley's and Jake Cousins' lives, yet he had left him his own just as Lije had left Prentiss his. Hot tears stung Lije's eyes as he put the pistol back into his belt.

After Prentiss had gone, Alice Tulley came below to kiss Lije and hold him briefly in her rocking embrace. She whispered to him, "He must have been a good man, a good man. Thank the Lord he spared you. We got to get you out of here. They don't harm us womenfolk, but they're coming around with torches and kerosene to set fire to all the buildings. Mrs. Cousins saw them down the street. We got to get you out. You wait down here till I tell you when it's safe to go."

Time seemed to stand still as Lije waited in the black

cellar until he heard her call down, *"Now,* son! Hurry on up!"

Lije ran out of the cellar fast, just as a half-drunken bushwhacker, who'd visited a saloon before starting to loot and burn, came trotting past him, a Union flag trailing on the ground behind his horse. Spotting Lije on the porch, he took aim at him and fired.

Lije felt a hideous pain in his left knee and fell forward onto the porch as the rider rode on, laughing.

"Lijah!" cried Alice Tulley as she ran through the house carrying a big red-and-brown oval rag rug. Mrs. Cousins ran behind her.

Lije couldn't speak. The pain was too severe.

"Be quiet, Lijah," ordered Sarah Mae Cousins. "We're going to roll you up in this rug, and that's where you're going to stay. The Rebs are out in front with kerosene right now."

Lije was rolled inside the rug, then rolled down the back steps behind the house. He could hear the women puffing and grunting as they pushed the heavy rug. A moment later, something heavy was placed on top of him. The women were taking their belongings outside to save them from the fire. How hot and stuffy it was inside the rug. He wanted to sneeze as dust from the carpet tickled his nose.

Though Lije couldn't see what was going on around him, he could hear and smell it. Pistol shots rang out nonstop amid wild yells of fear and whoops of joy. He could smell the burning houses and stores and hear the crackling of flames. God in heaven, Quantrill was killing Lawrence! He'd sack it for anything of value, rob the banks, murder its leading men citizens, and leave it in cinders.

Tears flooded Lije's eyes. He'd failed to warn the town. He should have got away from Jesse and got here sooner. He wept silently from his pain and helpless fury, and for his anguish over the fate of the town and its people. He knew Quantrill would be gunning down every known Jayhawker he could ferret out, and plenty of other men and boys besides. The bushwhackers had boasted of it all along their ride.

Suddenly, during a lull in the din, Lije heard singing. Had he gone mad? No, it was his mother singing a lullaby. He guessed at her meaning in her words, "Rest. Go to sleep, my darling. I'm here."

Lije lay in the rug for nearly four hours. By eight, the August heat had begun. He sweltered, half suffocated, and sometimes lost consciousness, but the pain in his knee brought him to awareness each time he dared move a bit. It ached. It throbbed. He couldn't put his hand down to touch it. He didn't dare change his position lest some bushwhacker see the rug move. Thirst began to torture him. He longed for a dipper of water. He could drink up half a well, he was so thirsty. He knew his mother would fetch him water if he whispered to her that he needed it, but he kept quiet. Her handing a cup to a rug would surely give them both away.

By eight-thirty, the smell of smoke had grown stronger. But the town was now quiet. Lije guessed why. The bushwhackers were robbing or visiting the saloons. That would occupy them for a while. He'd never known one who didn't love whiskey, even Jim Hickok. Where was he now? Where was Ira?

All at once, Lije felt a deep, heavy thudding. That meant running horses, many running horses. Had the Union army come, or more bushwhackers?

Now he heard his mother's voice say softly at the end of the rug near his head, "Lijah, they're leaving. The Army's coming. Don't move. Speak to me, son."

"Ma," was all he could manage to get out before he lost consciousness once more.

He didn't know where he was when he awakened. He was in a strange bed under a red-and-white quilt and in a strange room. His mother was bending over him.

"You're fine, Lijah," she told him. "You been here two whole days. This is a brick house. Quantrill couldn't burn it down. The doctor's been here. He got the bullet out of your knee. You lost a lot of blood."

Lije managed to ask, "Ira? Is he dead?"

"No, thank the Lord. He went to Fort Leavenworth with his uncle last week to visit someone."

Lije closed his eyes, more weak and weary than he'd ever been in his life. He asked, eyes closed, "Mr. Montgomery and Dr. Jennison—did the bushwhackers kill them, too?"

"No, they weren't here either. Quantrill's men burned a hundred houses, and killed our men and boys wherever they could find them, curse the devils. Then they ran away. The U.S. Cavalry's chasing them right now."

Lije whispered, "I wish I was chasing them, too."

Mrs. Tulley sat down in the chair beside the bed. "The doctor says you won't be riding anywhere for a good long time, Lijah, and you'll probably always walk with a limp. Your kneecap got smashed. He says the war's over for you. I've been told of the spy work you did. That was brave of you, Elijah, and I'm proud of you. So would Pa be."

Lija sighed. "Well, Ma, I did try. I guess I didn't do so good, did I?"

"Yes, you did, for someone who just turned sixteen. There's somebody here who can tell you that better than I can, though."

Saying that, Mrs. Tulley rose, bent down to kiss Lije on the forehead, and left.

He closed his eyes. It'd probably be Montgomery or Jennison expecting a report from him. He'd tell whoever it was that he'd tell him tomorrow—he was too weary now.

His visitor wasn't either of them, though. Lije could tell that by the light, quick step on the creaking floor.

His eyes opened to see Mary Dent standing beside him, smiling. She wore red ribbons in her hair and a red gingham dress.

"Mary!"

He tried to sit up, but she pushed him back.

"How come you're here?"

"Ma and I live here. This is my grandma's house. We were taken out of Missouri on Mr. Hickok's orders. We were glad to go."

"I guess you're done with spying, too."

"I reckon so. Ma and I did our duty by the North. She took your messages to Keytesville in baskets of eggs, and they were passed on to Lawrence. Mr. Montgomery told me I did real fine work and said you did, too. He said we were good Jayhawkers."

"Is that how you did it—in egg baskets?"

She smiled. "We had to be sure to sell them to the right folks. Your ma says you can't go off and join the Union army with that bad knee. I'm sorry you got hurt, but I'm glad you can't go." She sat down. "I'd say we did enough, and so does Mr. Montgomery."

"Were you here when Quantrill came?"

"You bet!" Her face grew dark with anger. "I could have shot him from my window I was so close to him one time, but Ma said no."

Lije asked, "Have you got Banner?"

"You bet I have. A drunk-as-sin bushwhacker tried to steal him out of Grandma's stable, but Banner fussed so, kicking and lashing at him with his hoofs, the man gave up and left."

"Good for Banner," said Lije. "What about Crow?"

"Crow was taken away with the bushwhackers. I seen somebody leading him. I'm sorry."

"I am, too. He was almost as good as Banner." Overcome with fatigue, Lije closed his eyes. He wished he could drink in Mary's dark loveliness, but he couldn't. Not now.

Seeing how weary Lije was, Mary told him, "Go to sleep now. I'll come back tomorrow."

Lije nodded and grinned. Then he felt her lips on his and went on smiling as her footsteps faded and the door closed quietly.

Images flashed through his mind now—Nettie Gaines, John Brown, Jim Hickok, Lotta, Quantrill and his bushwhackers. He relived the horror of Wilson's Creek, then burning houses and galloping horses, and the wonder of what had happened down in the root cellar between him and Prentiss—the man he had spared and who had spared him.

His war looked to be over. Yet in his way he reckoned he'd helped to stop slavery from going on, hadn't he? But maybe the doctor had been wrong. Maybe he'd get well faster than he'd thought. If he did, he would go out hunting Quantrill on Banner. Maybe he'd find Crow and fetch him home to Kansas. That was a lot of maybe's, but thinking "maybe" didn't cost anything, and it surely did comfort.

Elijah Tulley fell asleep with a smile on his face.

Author's Note

Though I have not written about it until now, the Civil War period in the Kansas-Missouri area has fascinated me since my childhood. My mother's family lived near Manhattan, Kansas, during that era. I grew up on tales of "bushwhackers" and "Jayhawkers." One of my great-great-grandfathers (his name was Absalom) was killed by invading Missourians during a Kansas territorial election riot—"stomped to death," as the legend goes. He was an abolitionist.

The War Between the States began in this region before it started nationwide in 1861. In the 1850s, abolitionists raided Missouri farms to "save" slaves. John Brown, who was in Kansas Territory in late 1858, was their martyred hero. Enraged Missourians retaliated by burning Kansas towns and farms. Outright murder was not at all uncommon, though it was strikingly true that white women were not shot down or attacked. (The same could not be said for black or Indian women, however.)

Life in eastern Kansas and Missouri between 1854 and 1865 must have been agonizing, not only because of the raiding and ferocious enmities, but because of the climate. Some seasons were brutal in the extreme. The summer of 1860, for instance, was long remembered for its severe drought and for such terrible heat that it drove settlers by the hundreds back to the northern states from which they had come. Noted Civil War historian E. B. Long once told me that, in his opinion, the Kansas pioneers were the "strongest, toughest, most courageous people America has ever produced." To honor them and the equally formidable Missourians, I have written *Jayhawker,* the tale of one farm boy who saw only his own small part of the horror that made his state known as "Bleeding Kansas."

THE PEOPLE IN THIS BOOK

The Tulley and Cousins families, the Prentisses, Lotta and her slaves, Judah Hamilton, Will Allen, Mr. Bass, Nettie Gaines, and Mary Dent are fictional. Other characters lived at the time. Using my research as my guide, I have described them as they actually looked and have written of them as I believe they would have acted and spoken.

THE JAYHAWKERS

John Brown was born in Connecticut in 1800. He grew up in Ohio, the son of a Bible-loving abolitionist who was a tanner by profession. Brown worked as a tanner and sheepman for some years. It was not until the age of fifty that he became so fervent an abolitionist, with visions of a huge slave rebellion in the South. In 1855, five of his sons went to Kansas as abolitionists, and Brown soon followed, bringing guns with him. In 1856, he and his sons fell upon five men who favored slavery and hacked them to death with swords. He left Kansas a hunted man, but returned in 1857 and in 1858, using the names of Shubel Morgan and Nelson Hawkins, and raided for slaves in Missouri. After his last raid, he set out for the East, bent on martyrdom. He went to Harpers Ferry, Virginia (now West Virginia), and seized the U.S. armory there in order to get weapons to arm slaves, who were then to rise up against their masters. U.S. Marines under the command of Colonel Robert E. Lee attacked his small force, killing some, wounding and capturing Brown. Tried and condemned, he was hanged on December 2, 1859. In the North, he was praised as a glorious hero; in the South, he was reviled. He is thought by some historians today to be an "inspired madman." Whatever he was, his actions inflamed public sentiment and contributed to the start of the Civil War.

No one could claim truly saintly behavior for the antislavery men who went out raiding. They burned, looted, shot, and hanged, too. Their cause may have been more just than that of slave-owning Southerners. However, their methods were decidedly not more genteel, and their courtesy to women was less marked than that of the bushwhackers.

James Montgomery was a fiery-natured, black-bearded man who came to Kansas from Ohio. He soon became a leader of the antislavery forces raiding Missouri farms. Instrumental in organizing the Jayhawker bands, he finally joined the Union army after some battles had been fought in Missouri.

Dr. Charles Jennison, a physician known for his elegant dress, came to Kansas around 1860 and worked with James Montgomery setting up vigilante groups. His riders were called "Redlegs" at times because of their red-topped boots. At the time of Quantrill's 1863 raid on Lawrence, he was at Fort Leavenworth. He became a colonel in the Union army and distinguished himself during the October 1864 battle of Westport, Kansas, the largest Civil War battle west of the Missouri River.

As for the name Jayhawker, it stems from a Kansas joke. It is a mythical bird. There is a sparrow hawk, but no jayhawk.

THE BUSHWHACKERS

Except for scattered instances, it is almost impossible to write of the exact whereabouts of specific members of Charley Quantrill's band between the years 1862 and 1865. Sources are vague or in disagreement, and biographical accounts by men who survived the Civil War understandably shade the truth to show themselves in a better light. It is fact, however, that bushwhacker (and Jayhawker) groups did not gather in any one place for long. Their custom was to disband after

a raid and return home, or go to safe houses or sometimes to caves, and wait to be summoned again to a
particular rendezvous. As happens in my book, riders
would come constantly to hideouts with not only orders from leaders, but with news of the war in other
parts of the United States. There were no telephones
then. Mail service was undependable, and the telegraph
lines had only been installed in a few communities.
Not every town had a newspaper. News traveled via
steamboats on the Missouri River and by riders.

Missouri mothers actually brought their sons to join
Quantrill's riders. Women relatives often sheltered the
partisans. To prevent this, the women were rounded
up in 1863 and jailed in various places or sent out of
the state. The collapse of the Kansas City jail that killed
kinswomen of Bill Anderson and the Younger brothers
is historical fact. It further inflamed the bushwhackers
and led to the attack on Lawrence.

William Quantrill (also called Charley or Billy) was
born in 1837 in Ohio, and has the unenviable distinc-
tion of being one of the most unsavory individuals in
American history. The son of a teacher and himself a
teacher for a few years, he had some education, but all
the same was notorious in his childhood for his cruelty.
There were criminal ancestors in his family. By 1860,
he had become a common criminal himself, robbing
and stealing horses. For a time in Kansas he passed
himself off as an abolitionist, while actually leading

men to their deaths on Missouri raids. Personally brave, he was at the battles of Wilson's Creek, Pea Ridge, and Prairie Grove. He raided Union-held towns and led the attack on Lawrence. Though he had been given an officer's rank by the Confederate government, regular soldiers disliked him and his bushwhackers. The Confederate colonel who joined him in attacking Lawrence actually said he "regretted participating." In 1864, Quantrill split company with his lieutenants after a quarrel. He set out for the East with thirty followers in a mad scheme to assassinate President Lincoln. (John Wilkes Booth accomplished that before he could try.) On May 10, 1865, Quantrill was wounded in a skirmish with Yankee troops not far from Louisville, Kentucky, was hospitalized there, and died at the age of twenty-seven. From 1888 to 1920, members of his partisans met annually at Blue Springs, Missouri, calling themselves "Confederate" veterans.

Jesse Woodson James, who is probably America's best known and most controversial outlaw, was born in Missouri in 1847. After his family suffered from outrages at the hands of Union men, Jesse joined his elder brother, Frank, as a bushwhacker some time in 1863, and took part in the battle of Prairie Grove. It is a matter of debate among folklorists whether or not Jesse was at Lawrence; certainly Frank James was. By 1864, Jesse was part of Bill Anderson's band, and in September of that year, he took part in a very brutal raid on Centralia, Missouri, where unarmed Union soldiers were massacred. Wounded, Jesse went to Texas, but returned to Missouri by the end of the war. Some historians believe that during this time he was sent home to his mother in Nebraska to die. He recovered, though, and supposedly spent four peaceful years at home with his brother. Then they embarked on a career of bank and train robberies in several states, crimes that were to make them notorious. Some have depicted them as Robin Hoods, others as cruel thugs. While living under an assumed name, Jesse James was shot dead by a former associate in St. Joseph, Missouri, in 1882.

Frank James, whose real name was Alexander Franklin James, was born in Missouri in 1843. Joining the Missouri "partisans" around 1862, he was present at the battles of Wilson's Creek and Prairie Grove and the Lawrence raid. He may have gone to Kentucky with Quantrill in 1864. At the end of the war, he surrendered to Union men, but in the 1870s he joined his brother and others of Quantrill's old band in a career as a robber. He and Jesse flourished in crime for over a decade. When Jesse was killed, Frank gave himself up to the governor of Missouri and went to prison. Unlike Jesse, Frank lived to a ripe age, touring in a Wild West show and dying in 1915. His last years were peaceful. All too aware of the legends springing up about him and Jesse, he once wrote to a friend, saying, "I found one of those cheap novels about me and Jesse.

There is no truth in them . . . we will not let our son Robbie read them. . . . A lot of robberies blamed on us we never did."

Coleman Younger (also called Cole or Bud) was the best known of the Younger brothers. Born in 1844, he was the son of a Missouri landowner, Colonel Younger, who was robbed and shot by Union men. The Younger home was burned, rebuilt, and burned again. In his youth, Cole rode with Quantrill throughout the war. After it ended, he robbed with the James brothers. Caught in an 1876 Minnesota robbery, he was pardoned. Later he appeared in Wild West shows with Frank James. Truly reformed from his lawless ways, he became a preacher and died in 1916, an old man.

William Anderson, born in 1840, was a native of Missouri. He moved to Kansas, but was forced out by abolitionists. By 1862, he had become a bushwhacker and with his two brothers rode with Quantrill. Outraged at the death of his womenfolk while in jail, he participated in the raid on Lawrence, and after it he merged his gang with Quantrill's. Anderson did not stay with him for long. He formed his own band again and continued raiding and killing.

Anderson, who became known as "Bloody Bill," was more savage than Quantrill. His men went on rampages in Carroll County, and in September 1864 rode to Centralia, Missouri, then held by Union forces.

There they slaughtered Union soldiers on furlough who were caught aboard a train. He sacked Danville in October and on the twenty-sixth of that month was shot dead while leading a charge against Union men near Albany, Missouri.

James Butler Hickok was born in Illinois in 1837. Readers knowledgeable in Western history may have guessed what name he is known by today. Yes, he *was* called "Wild Bill Hickok," although he did not get that name until after the Civil War. A soft-spoken, easy-going dandy, but a dead shot, he hated slavery. His family had helped slaves escape on the Underground Railroad. Coming to Kansas in 1856, he drove a stage-coach from 1859 to 1860. In 1861, he allegedly became a scout for the Union army and part-time spy among the bushwhackers, who never suspected his real sympathies. He was at the Battle of Wilson's Creek and could have been at Pea Ridge, Arkansas, on the Union side. His Civil War years are shadowy and full of controversy, but most historians seem to agree he was a Union agent. He loved jokes, music, and children. His befriending of my Lije Tulley would have been in character. Hickok, who became a lawman in the territories farther to the west, did not grow old. In 1876, he was shot in the back during a saloon poker game in Deadwood, a frontier town in what is now South Dakota.

Largely rural Missouri seceded from the Union in November 1861, months after the Civil War began.

More than 1,160 battles and skirmishes were fought inside this state, and it was the center of much partisan activity, as well as formal military action. To show how divided the sympathies of its citizens were, consider the fact that 40,000 of its men wore "Confederate gray" and 110,000 wore "Union blue." One of the state's first actions in the war took place on May 10, 1861, and the last one on October 31, 1864. Large areas of embattled Missouri could find themselves under the control of the Confederates one year and the next year under Union forces. Travel was difficult. Roads were bad and railroads few, and rivers sometimes almost impassable because of bad weather.

THE LAWRENCE RAID

Without doubt, the August 1863 raid on Lawrence, Kansas, by proslavery men was one of the most terrible actions of the entire Civil War. The town, founded in 1854 by fervent abolitionists, most of them from Massachusetts, had been raided before. However, the May 1856 attack had consisted chiefly of looting. When Quantrill's partisans rode in in 1863, they looked in particular for prominent men. Whenever they found one, they shot him on the spot. The men of Lawrence were pursued in their homes, hotels, stores, stables, sheds, and cornfields. Some hid and escaped death. An abolitionist minister who hid in his cellar was saved by the quick thinking of his wife. When bushwhackers

set fire to their house, she rolled him in a rug out-
doors, then set furniture on top of him. Bushwhackers
looted all the stores and burned every wooden building on Massachusetts, the main street, destroying one
hundred eighty-five buildings in all. No woman or girl
was killed, but one hundred eighty-three men and
youths died, some shot down in their wives' and mothers' arms. Only one bushwhacker died after he was left
behind drunk when Quantrill rode out four hours later
to escape pursuing Union army cavalry.

Of course, John Brown's raids for slaves and those
of other abolitionists are factual, as is the existence of
the Underground Railroad to the North to freedom.
Lije's careful distancing of himself from Missouri slaves
would be necessary. He could not befriend them
openly or he would have been suspect. Slaves rev-
erenced and loved John Brown and did indeed name
him "Moses" as the man they hoped would lead them
out of captivity.

The parts Elijah Tulley and Mary Dent play in this
book may surprise some readers. They may seem too
young for the work they do. Americans do not send
children to war in this century. That was not true of
the last century. Drummer boys and buglers under the
age of twelve served in both the Union and Confederate armies, and distinguished themselves in combat.
Much more was expected of rural children then. A big
thirteen-year-old boy would sometimes do a man's

farm labor, and a girl would keep a house. Maturity was thrust early on children in a largely agricultural society where there was less leisure than today and every pair of hands could be needed to keep the farm and family going—no matter how small the hands.

In reading about the Civil War period in Kansas and Missouri, I was amazed to learn of other distinguished individuals who were there in the 1860s. Among them were "Buffalo Bill," William Cody; abolitionist newspaper editor Dan Anthony (father of Susan B. Anthony); Senator Jim Lane, another Jayhawker of note; and Samuel Clemens, later to become "Mark Twain," who served as a soldier in the Confederate Army.

One of my chief sources among many references for *Jayhawker* was Jay Monaghan's *Civil War on the Western Border 1854–1865,* Bonanza Books, New York, 1940. Three persons in particular have aided me in my research: Judy Sweets, of the Douglas County Historical Society, Lawrence, Kansas; Muriel Shields of Pensacola, Florida; and Professor Melbourne Evans of Albuquerque, New Mexico. Ms. Shields and Professor Evans are brother and sister, and are great-great-grandchildren of John Brown.